PENGUIN PLAYS

THE JUST and THE POSSESSED

Albert Camus was born in Algeria in 1913 of Breton and Spanish parentage. He was brought up in North Africa and had many jobs there (one of them playing in goal for the Algiers football team) before he came to Metropolitan France and took up journalism. He was active in the resistance during the German occupation and became editor of the clandestine paper *Combat*. Before the war he had written a play *Caligula* (1939), and during the war the two books which brought him fame, *L'Étranger* (*The Outsider*, 1942) and *Le Mythe de Sisyphe* (1942). Abandoning politics and journalism he devoted himself to writing and established an international reputation with such books as *La Peste* (*The Plague*, 1947), *Les Justes* (1949), *L'Homme révolté* (1952), and *La Chute* (*The Fall*, 1956). He was awarded the Nobel Prize for Literature in 1957. In January 1960 he was killed in a road accident.

ALBERT CAMUS

THE JUST

Translated by Henry Jones

THE POSSESSED

Translated by Justin O'Brien

PENGUIN BOOKS

Penguin Books Ltd, Harmondsworth, Middlesex, England
Penguin Books Australia Ltd, Ringwood, Victoria, Australia

—

Published in Penguin Books 1970

—

Made and printed in Great Britain by
C. Nicholls & Company Ltd
Set in Monotype Baskerville

Contents

THE JUST

A Play in Five Acts

Translated from the French by
HENRY JONES

Characters in the Play

DORA DOULEBOV
BORIS ANNENKOV *(Boria)*
STEPAN FEDOROV
ALEXIS VOINOV
IVAN KALIAYEV *(Yanek)*
GUARD
FOKA
SKOURATOV, *Chief of Police*
GRAND-DUCHESS

The action takes place in Moscow. The year – 1906.

ACT ONE

Scene: The terrorists' flat. The morning sun is shining through a window. When the curtain rises, DORA DOULEBOV *and* BORIS ANNENKOV *are standing in the middle of the room. Silence. Then the front-door bell rings once.* DORA *seems about to say something, but* ANNENKOV *signals to her to keep quiet. Two more rings in quick succession ...*

ANNENKOV: It's him! [*Exits ...* DORA *waits motionless; ...* ANNENKOV *returns with* STEPAN FEDOROV, *whom he clasps affectionately by the shoulders.*] Here he is! It's Stepan, he's back!

DORA [*going up to* STEPAN *and clasping his hand*]: Welcome home, Stepan!

STEPAN: Hello, Dora.

DORA: Three years – just think. [*She is gazing at him.*]

STEPAN: Yes ... three long years. The day they arrested me I was coming to join you.

DORA: Yes, we were expecting you all the time. I shall never forget how my heart sank as the minutes ticked away. We didn't dare look at each other.

ANNENKOV: Of course we had to move to another flat immediately.

STEPAN: I know.

DORA: How was it inside, Stepan?

STEPAN: Inside?

DORA: I mean in prison.

STEPAN: You can sometimes escape.

ANNENKOV: You know how we felt when we heard you'd got through to Switzerland.

STEPAN: Switzerland's a prison too.

ANNENKOV: Well, at least they're free there.

STEPAN: 'Freedom' will remain a prison until every man on earth is free! I was free of course, but all I could think about were Russia and ... her slaves. [*Short pause.*]

ANNENKOV: I'm glad they've sent you here.

STEPAN: I had to come. I was suffocating. At least I can do something. [*Looks at* ANNENKOV.] We *are* going to kill him, aren't we?

ANNENKOV: Yes we are.

STEPAN: We'll kill the murderer....You're the one who gives the orders, Boria, and I will always obey you.

ANNENKOV: I don't need any promises, Stepan. We are all brothers.

STEPAN: We must have discipline. That's one thing I did learn in prison. The Socialist Revolution must have discipline. Then we will kill the Grand Duke and crush tyranny for ever.

DORA [*going towards him*]: Sit down, Stepan. You must be tired after your long journey.

STEPAN: I'm never tired. [*A pause* ... DORA *sits.*] Is everything ready, Boria?

ANNENKOV [*changing tone*]: For the last month, two of our men have been studying the Duke's movements. Dora has got together all the materials we need.

STEPAN: Has the proclamation been drafted yet?

ANNENKOV: Yes. All Russia shall know that the Socialist Revolutionary party has killed the Grand Duke Sergei to hasten the liberation of the Russian people. The Imperial Court will learn that we are determined to continue our reign of terror until the land is returned to the people.

Yes, Stepan, everything is ready! We haven't long to wait.

STEPAN: What's my job?

ANNENKOV: To begin with, you will help Dora. You'll replace Schweitzer, who used to work with her.

STEPAN: He was killed, was he?

ANNENKOV: Yes.

STEPAN: How?

DORA: An accident. [STEPAN *looks at* DORA, *who lowers her gaze.*]

STEPAN: What do I do after that?

ANNENKOV: We'll see about that later. You must be ready as a replacement, if necessary, and you must make sure that we keep in contact with Headquarters.

STEPAN: Who are our friends here?

ANNENKOV: You met Voinov in Switzerland. He's young but thoroughly reliable. Then there's Yanek . . . you don't know him, do you?

STEPAN: Yanek?

ANNENKOV: His real name is Kaliayev. We also called him the 'Poet'.

STEPAN: That's no name for a terrorist.

ANNENKOV [*laughing*]: Well, Yanek thinks it is. He says that all poetry is revolutionary.

STEPAN: Only bombs are revolutionary . . . [*A pause.*]. . . . Do you think I'll be able to help you, Dora?

DORA: Oh yes! You'll have to be careful when you're handling the fuse though.

STEPAN: What if it breaks?

DORA: That's how Schweitzer was killed. [*A pause.*] What are you smiling at, Stepan?

STEPAN: Was I smiling?

DORA: Yes, you were.

STEPAN: I do ... sometimes. [*A pause.*] Tell me, Dora, would one bomb be enough to blow up this house?

DORA: Not one by itself, but it would do a lot of damage.

STEPAN: How many bombs would it take to blow up Moscow?

ANNENKOV: Are you out of your mind? What do you mean?

STEPAN: Oh, nothing ... [*Slight pause, the bell rings once ... they wait, listening ... the bell rings twice ...* ANNENKOV *goes through into the hall and returns with* ALEXIS VOINOV.]

VOINOV: Stepan!

STEPAN: Hello, Alexis. [*They shake hands ...* VOINOV *then goes to* DORA *and embraces her.*]

ANNENKOV: Everything all right, Alexis?

VOINOV: Yes.

ANNENKOV: Have you studied the route from the palace to the theatre?

VOINOV: I can map it out for you now. [*He takes out a sheet of paper from his jacket and draws.*] Look. Turnings, narrow streets, crossroads ... the carriage will go by under our window.

ANNENKOV: What do those two crosses mean?

VOINOV: One is a little square where the horses will have to slow down; the other is the theatre, where they'll stop. Those are the best places, I think.

ANNENKOV: Right – give it to me.

STEPAN: What about police spies?

VOINOV [*hesitantly*]: They're all over the place.

STEPAN: They worry you, do they?

VOINOV: Well, I'm not very happy about them.

ANNENKOV: Nobody is. Don't worry, Alexis.

VOINOV: It's not that I'm afraid; I'm just not used to lying, that's all.

STEPAN: Everybody lies. The important thing is to lie well.

VOINOV: It's not so easy. When I was at University, the other students always laughed at me, because I could never hide my feelings. I always blurted everything out. I was expelled in the end.

STEPAN: Why?

VOINOV: In my history course, my tutor asked me how Peter the Great founded Petrograd...

STEPAN: Good question.

VOINOV: I said that he founded it on murder and brutality. In the end I was expelled.

STEPAN: And what then?

VOINOV: Then I realized that it wasn't enough just to denounce injustice. One must give one's life to fighting it. So, now I'm happy.

STEPAN: And yet you have to lie.

VOINOV: I do *now*, yes. But I'll have finished lying on the day I throw the bomb ... [*The bell rings – twice and then once ...* DORA *gets up with a start.*]

ANNENKOV: It's Yanek. [DORA *rushes out.*]

STEPAN: It was a different signal.

ANNENKOV: Oh, it's just one of Yanek's whims. He has his private signal ... [STEPAN *shrugs his shoulders ...* DORA'S *voice is heard in the hall ...* DORA *and* IVAN KALIAYEV *come in, arm in arm ...* KALIAYEV *is laughing.*]

DORA: Yanek, this is Stepan – he's replacing Schweitzer.

KALIAYEV: Welcome, Stepan!

STEPAN: Thank you. [DORA *and* KALIAYEV *both sit down, facing the others.*]

ANNENKOV: You'll recognize the carriage, Yanek?

KALIAYEV: Yes. I've had two long looks at it and I'd recognize it a mile off! I've noted every detail – one of the panes of the left-hand lamp is chipped, for instance.

VOINOV: What about police spies?

KALIAYEV [*laughing*]: Oh, they're all over the place, but we're old friends – I sell them cigarettes!!

ANNENKOV: Has Pavel confirmed our information?

KALIAYEV: The Grand Duke is due to go to the theatre this week. Pavel will soon know the exact day . . . he'll leave a message at the door . . . [*Turning to* DORA *and laughing.*] Oh, Dora, we're in luck.

DORA [*looking at him*]: I see you've taken off your peddlar's outfit. You're a proper gentleman now! You look quite handsome! Don't you miss your fluffy coat?

KALIAYEV [*laughing*]: I certainly do . . . I was very proud of it. [*To* STEPAN *and* ANNENKOV.] First I spent two months watching the peddlars at work, then another month or so practising in my room. They never suspected a thing. 'He's amazing,' they used to say. 'He'd sell the Tsar's horses and get away with it!' In fact, they tried to pick up a few hints!

DORA: And of course you laughed.

KALIAYEV: You know I can't help laughing. The disguise, the new life . . . everything amused me.

DORA: I can't bear fancy-dress. [*Pointing to her dress.*] And then, this luxurious get-up! Boria might have found something else. Me! An actress? No, I'm *simple*-hearted.

KALIAYEV [*laughing*]: But you look so pretty in it.

DORA: Pretty? I'd like to be pretty, but I mustn't think about that . . .

KALIAYEV: Oh, Dora! Why not? There is always such a sad look in your eyes. You should be full of joy and pride. . . . There *is* beauty and happiness in the world! 'In those quiet places where my heart once longed for you . . .'

DORA [*smiling*]: ' . . . I breathed eternal summer.'

KALIAYEV: Oh, Dora! You remember those lines . . . and you're smiling. Oh, I'm so happy!

STEPAN [*cutting in*]: We're wasting our time. Boria, hadn't we better go down and see the porter? [KALIAYEV *looks at* STEPAN *with bewilderment.*]

ANNENKOV: Yes. Would you go down, Dora? . . . and don't forget the tip. Then Alexis will help you get the stuff together in the other room. [DORA *and* VOINOV *exit . . .* STEPAN *walks quickly up to* ANNENKOV.]

STEPAN: I want to throw the bomb.

ANNENKOV: No, Stepan. It's already been decided.

STEPAN: I beg you to let me throw the bomb. You know how much it means to me.

ANNENKOV: No, orders are orders. [*A pause.*] I'm not throwing the bomb either . . . I'll be waiting here too; it's hard, but those are the rules.

STEPAN: Who *is* going to throw the first bomb?

KALIAYEV: I am . . . and Voinov's throwing the second one.

STEPAN: You!

KALIAYEV: Yes. Does it surprise you? Don't you trust me?

STEPAN: It's a matter of experience.

KALIAYEV: Experience? You know you can only throw the bomb once . . . and then . . . no one's ever had a second chance.

STEPAN: You need a steady hand.

KALIAYEV [*holding out his hand*]: Look! Do you think that hand will tremble? [STEPAN *turns round.*] No, it won't tremble. Do you think that I shall hesitate when the Grand Duke's there in front of me? Surely you cannot think that! [STEPAN *turns his back on* KALIAYEV.] And even if my arm did begin to tremble . . . I know a sure way of killing him.

STEPAN: What's that?

KALIAYEV: I'd throw myself under the horses' feet.

[STEPAN *shrugs his shoulders, walks to the back of the room and sits.*]

ANNENKOV: There won't be any need for that. Your orders are to try to get away. The Organization needs you – you save yourself if you can.

KALIAYEV: All right, Boria, but what an honour for me and I shall live up to it!

ANNENKOV: Stepan ... you will be in the street while Yanek and Alexis are waiting for the carriage. I want you to walk up and down in front of our window at regular intervals – we'll settle on a signal later. Dora and I will wait here and issue the proclamation when the time comes. With a bit of luck the Grand Duke will be dead.

KALIAYEV [*triumphantly*]: Yes, I shall kill him ... and how glorious it will be if it is successful! But, of course, the Grand Duke is nothing ... we must strike higher.

ANNENKOV: But we must start with the Grand Duke.

KALIAYEV: And suppose we fail, Boria ... then we must do what the Japanese did.

ANNENKOV: What do you mean?

KALIAYEV: During the war, the Japanese never surrendered ... they killed themselves!

ANNENKOV: No, Yanek, don't think of suicide.

KALIAYEV: What should I think of then?

ANNENKOV: Of carrying on our work of terrorism.

STEPAN [*still facing the back of the room*]: To commit suicide, a man must have a great love for himself. A true revolutionary cannot love himself.

KALIAYEV [*turning on* STEPAN ... *sharply*]: A true revolutionary? Why are you treating me like this ... what have you got against me?

STEPAN: I don't like people who dabble with revolution because they're bored.

ANNENKOV: Stepan!

STEPAN [*gets up and walks down towards them*]: Yes, I'm brutal ... but for me hatred is not just a game. We aren't here to admire each other ... we are here to succeed.

KALIAYEV [*in a soft voice*]: Why are you taking it out on me? Who told you that I was bored?

STEPAN: There was no need to tell me. You change the signals. You like dressing up as a peddlar. You recite poems and now you want to throw yourself under the horses' feet. [*A pause* ... STEPAN *looks at* KALIAYEV.] No, I can't say you inspire me with confidence.

KALIAYEV [*louder*]: You don't know me, brother. I love life and I'm never bored. I joined the revolution *because* I love life!

STEPAN: I don't love life ... I love something higher than mere life ... I love justice.

KALIAYEV [*with visible restraint*]: Each of us serves justice in his own way – you in yours and I in mine. Why not agree to be different? Let's love one another if we can.

STEPAN: We cannot.

KALIAYEV [*shouting*]: What are you doing with us then?

STEPAN: I have come to kill a man, not to love him or agree to differ from him.

KALIAYEV [*passionately*]: You will not kill him by yourself... for no cause! You will kill him with us ... on behalf of the Russian people! That is your only justification.

STEPAN [*furiously*]: I don't need any justification! I got all the justification I'll ever want three years ago, one night in prison ... and I won't put up with ...

ANNENKOV: That's enough! Are you both out of your minds? Have you forgotten who we are? We are all brothers working hand in hand to put an end to tyranny and set our people free! *Together*, we will kill, and nothing can divide us! [*Silence ... he looks at them.*] Come along,

Stepan ... we must settle the signals. [*Exit* STEPAN.] Don't take it to heart, Yanek. Stepan has been through a lot ... I'll have a word with him.

KALIAYEV [*he is very pale*]: He insulted me, Boria. [*Enter* DORA.]

DORA [*seeing* KALIAYEV]: What's wrong?

ANNENKOV: Nothing. [*He exits.*]

DORA [*to* KALIAYEV]: What's wrong, Yanek?

KALIAYEV: We've had a row already. He doesn't like me. [DORA *sits in silence ... a pause.*]

DORA: I don't think he likes anyone, but he'll be happier when it's all over. Don't worry, Yanek.

KALIAYEV: But I *do* worry. I want you all to love me. I've sacrificed everything for the Organization and I couldn't bear it if my brothers turned away from me. Sometimes I feel they don't understand me. Perhaps it's my fault ... I know I often don't say the right things and I ...

DORA: They *do* love you ... they *do* understand you; only Stepan is different.

KALIAYEV: No, Dora. I know what he thinks. Schweitzer used to say the same sort of thing: 'Yanek! Yanek's too eccentric to be a revolutionary ...' If only I could convince them I'm not eccentric. They think I'm a bit mad, too impulsive, but I believe in our cause just as they do. I am ready to lay down my life for it like them! *I* can be cunning and cool, secretive and efficient ... only I am still convinced that life is a glorious thing – love ... beauty ... and happiness. That's why I hate tyranny! But how can I explain it to them? Revolution – yes! ... but revolution for the sake of life – to give life a chance ... do *you* understand?

DORA: Yes, I understand! ... [*Pause ... more softly*] ... but what we're giving is not life ... but death.

KALIAYEV: We? ... Oh, I see what you mean. No, that's not the same thing at all. We are killing to build a world where there'll be no killing at all. We must accept our role as criminals, until finally everyone on earth is innocent...

DORA: Suppose it doesn't work out like that?

KALIAYEV: No, Dora! You know that's impossible. Stepan would be right then... and we'd have to spit in the face of beauty.

DORA: I've been in the Organization longer than you have and I know that nothing is as simple as you think. But you have faith ... and faith is what we all need.

KALIAYEV: Faith? [*Long pause.*] No ... no, only one man had that...

DORA: You have conviction in your soul. You will push aside everything to fulfil your ideal. Why did you ask to throw the first bomb?

KALIAYEV: Can you just talk about revolution without actually taking part in it? [*He begins to pace about.*]

DORA: No...

KALIAYEV: No, you must be right at the heart of it all.

DORA [*thoughtfully*]: Yes ... there you are, right out in front ... and then the final moment – that's what we must think of. That's when we need courage and inspiration.

KALIAYEV: I've thought of nothing else for a year. This is the moment I've been waiting for all my life, and I now know that I would die right there beside the Grand Duke ... I would shed my blood to the very last drop or shrivel up in the heat of the explosion. Do you understand why I asked to throw the first bomb? To die for our ideal – it's the only way to prove myself worthy of it ... it's the only justification.

DORA: I would like to die like that too.

KALIAYEV: It's the greatest happiness one could wish for ... and yet ... sometimes, at night, when I'm lying awake on a thin straw mattress – that's all a peddlar can afford – sometimes it worries me to think that they have forced us to be murderers ... but then I remember that I am going to die too ... and everything's all right. I smile to myself ... like a child, and go back to sleep again.

DORA: That's how it should be, Yanek – to kill and to die ... but I think there is an even greater happiness ... [*a pause*] ... [*lowering her gaze as* KALIAYEV *looks at her*] ... the scaffold.

KALIAYEV [*fervently*]: I have thought about that too.... Yes, there's something incomplete about dying on the spot ... but between that moment and the scaffold, there is an eternity ... perhaps the only eternity man can ever know.

DORA [*she is intense and eager ... she takes his hands in hers*]: That's the thought that will help you through: we are giving more than we take.

KALIAYEV: What do you mean?

DORA: We are forced to kill, aren't we? We deliberately sacrifice a life, don't we? A single life?

KALIAYEV: Yes.

DORA: But throwing a bomb and then climbing the scaffold ... that's giving one's life twice ... so we give more than we take.

KALIAYEV: Yes ... that's dying twice. Thank you, Dora. No one can reproach us for anything now ... now I am sure of myself! [*A pause.*] What is it, Dora?

DORA: I'd like to help you more ... only ...

KALIAYEV: Only what?

DORA: No, I mustn't.

KALIAYEV: Don't you trust me?

DORA: Darling, it's myself I don't trust. Since Schweitzer died, some strange thoughts have occurred to me ... but it's not for me to tell you what will be difficult.

KALIAYEV: I like things that are difficult. If you *respect* me at all, you will tell me.

DORA [*looking at him*]: I know. You are very brave. That's what worries me. You laugh, you work yourself up, you go forward eagerly to the sacrifice ... but in a few hours, you will have to come out of your dream and face reality. Perhaps it's best to talk about this before, so that there is no surprise, no possibility of flinching.

KALIAYEV: I shall not falter! ... but please ... carry on.

DORA: Throwing the bomb, the scaffold, dying twice over – that's the easy part. Your heart will see you through ... but you'll be standing right out in front ... [*she looks at him and seems to hesitate*] ... and you'll see him.

KALIAYEV: See who?

DORA: The Grand Duke.

KALIAYEV: Yes, but only for a moment.

DORA: In that moment, you'll look at him.... Oh, Yanek, it's best for you to know, to be warned. A man is a man – the Grand Duke may have gentle eyes. Perhaps you'll see him smiling to himself or scratching his ear. Perhaps, who knows, you'll see a little scar on his cheek where he cut himself shaving ... and if he looks at you at the moment ...

KALIAYEV: It's not him I'm destroying ... I'm destroying tyranny!

DORA: Yes, I know; tyranny must be destroyed.... I'll get the bomb ready, and when I'm screwing in the tube – that's the moment when it's touch and go, when one's nerves are all on edge ... and yet I'll feel strangely happy ... but then I don't know the Grand Duke. It wouldn't be nearly so easy, if he was sitting in front of me while I was screwing in the tube, looking at me ... but *you will* see him ... he'll be quite near you, just a yard or two away.

KALIAYEV [*passionately*]: I shall not see him!

DORA: Why? ... are you going to shut your eyes?

KALIAYEV: No ... but with God's help, my ... hatred will surge up just in time and blind me! [*The bell rings once ... they do not move ...* STEPAN *and* VOINOV *enter ... voices are heard in the hall ... enter* ANNENKOV.]

ANNENKOV [*a pause*]: It's the porter. The Grand Duke is going to the theatre ... tomorrow! [*He looks at them all.*] Everything must be ready, Dora.

DORA [*in a low voice*]: Right. [*Exit* DORA.]

KALIAYEV [*watches her go ... then, turning to* STEPAN, *in a quiet voice*]: I shall kill him ... with joy!

CURTAIN

ACT TWO

Scene: The same . . . the following evening. ANNENKOV *is looking out of the window.* DORA *is standing by the table.*

ANNENKOV: Yanek and Alexis are ready. Stepan has just lit a cigarette.

DORA: When is the Grand Duke due to go by?

ANNENKOV: Any minute now. Listen! . . . isn't that a carriage? No . . .

DORA: Be patient, Boria. Sit down.

ANNENKOV: What about the bombs?

DORA: Do sit down – there's nothing more we can do.

ANNENKOV: Yes, there is – we can envy them . . .

DORA: You belong here: you're in charge.

ANNENKOV: Yes, I'm in charge, but Yanek's a better man; perhaps he's the one . . .

DORA: The risk is the same for everyone – for the man who throws the bomb and the man who doesn't.

ANNENKOV: In the long run, yes, the risk is the same, but today it is Yanek and Alexis who are in the firing line. Oh, I know I haven't the right to be with them, but sometimes I can't help thinking that perhaps I'm a little too ready to play my part. After all, it's much easier not to have to throw the bomb yourself.

DORA: What if it is? The only thing that really matters is that you do your duty to the end.

ANNENKOV: Oh, you're so calm, Dora!

DORA: I'm not calm: I'm frightened! I've been with the Group for three years, and for two years I've been making the bombs. I have done everything I was told to do, and I don't think I've ever let you down....

ANNENKOV: Of course you haven't, Dora...

DORA: Well... all those three years... I've been afraid. I've been haunted by that creeping fear that leaves you only when you go to sleep; but when you wake up, there it is waiting at your bedside... so I just had to get used to it. I've trained myself to keep calm just when I'm most afraid. But it's nothing to be proud of.

ANNENKOV: You should be proud. Look at me... I've never really mastered anything. You know... I sometimes find myself regretting the old days... the gay life, pretty women... yes, I used to enjoy the drinking... and the women, and those nights that went on for ever....

DORA: I always thought so, Boria! That's why I'm so fond of you; you still have a heart, even if it still longs for pleasure.... Surely that is better than the awful coldness that sometimes stifles all emotion.

ANNENKOV: Dora, what are you saying? Is it possible? Hearing that from you!

DORA [*standing up abruptly as the sound of a carriage passing by is heard*]: Ssh! Listen! [*Silence.*] No, it isn't him; my heart is pounding. You see... I've still a lot to learn.

ANNENKOV [*going to the window*]: Hold it! Stepan's signalling... It's him! He's coming!... [*They listen to the distant rumbling of a carriage, which draws nearer and nearer and then goes by the window... a long silence...*] In a few seconds... [*a pause*]... oh, how time drags. What can have happened? [DORA *flinches... long silence... church bells are heard in the distance.*] Oh, no! Yanek should have thrown the bomb by now. The carriage must have reached the theatre. What about Alexis? Look! Stepan's running back towards the theatre.

DORA [*flinging herself against* ANNENKOV]: Yanek's been arrested! They've arrested him ... they have, they have! Oh, Boria, we must do something!

ANNENKOV: Wait ... [*He listens.*] No... well, that's it then.

DORA: How did it happen? How can Yanek have been arrested when he hasn't done anything? He was ready for it, I know he was: he wanted the prison and the trial... but after he had killed the Grand Duke ... not like this ... oh, no, not like this! [ANNENKOV *glances outside.*]

ANNENKOV: It's Alexis ... quickly ... [DORA *rushes to the door and opens it to reveal* VOINOV *looking distraught.*] What's happened, Alexis? What's happened?

VOINOV: I don't know ... I was waiting for the first bomb ... I ... I saw the carriage rounding the corner ... and nothing happened ... I panicked ... I thought you'd changed the plans at the last minute ... and I hesitated ... and ... and then I ran back here.

ANNENKOV: What about Yanek?

VOINOV: I haven't seen him.

DORA: He *has* been arrested!

ANNENKOV [*looking out of the window*]: No ... there he is!

[KALIAYEV *comes in, tears streaming down his face.*]

KALIAYEV [*distraught*]: Forgive me ... I ... I couldn't do it. ... [DORA *goes to him and takes his hand.*]

DORA: It's all right, Yanek ... it's all right ...

ANNENKOV: What happened?

DORA: Don't worry, Yanek – it's like that sometimes; at the last minute everything goes wrong.

ANNENKOV: No, I can't believe it!

DORA: Leave him alone. You're not the only one, Yanek – Schweitzer couldn't pull it off the first time either.

ANNENKOV: Were you afraid?

KALIAYEV [*with a start*]: Afraid! No! ... you've got no right to. . . . [*The bell rings once and then twice . . . they all stand quite still . . . at a signal from* ANNENKOV, VOINOV *goes out . . .* KALIAYEV *is crushed . . . silence . . . enter* STEPAN.]

ANNENKOV: Well?

STEPAN: There were children in the Grand Duke's carriage.

ANNENKOV: Children!

STEPAN: Yes . . . his nephew and niece.

ANNENKOV: Orlov said the Grand Duke would be alone.

STEPAN: The Grand Duchess was there as well: too many people for our poet, I suppose! Luckily, the police-spies didn't notice anything. [ANNENKOV *speaks quietly to* STEPAN *. . . they all watch* KALIAYEV, *who stares at* STEPAN.]

KALIAYEV [*dazed*]: I never thought it would be like that . . . children . . . oh no, not children! Have you ever looked at a child and seen those grave, intent eyes? . . . somehow I can never face them . . . and to think that only a moment before I was so gloriously happy . . . standing on the corner of that little side-street . . . in a patch of shadow. . . . The moment I saw the carriage lights shining in the distance, my heart began to race, with joy . . . yes, with joy. . . . It beat faster and faster as the rumbling of the wheels drew nearer . . . I wanted to leap in the air . . . I really believe . . . I was laughing and I kept on saying, 'Yes . . . Yes!' . . . do you understand? [*He looks away from* STEPAN *and sinks again into depression.*] I ran forward! . . . it was then that I saw the children. [*A pause.*] *They* weren't laughing . . . just staring in front of them, holding themselves . . . very straight. How sad they looked! . . . swamped in their best clothes, their hands resting on their thighs, like two little statues framed in the windows on each side of the door . . . I didn't see the Grand Duchess . . . I only saw them. If they had looked at me then I think I would have thrown the bomb, if only to shut out the sad look in their eyes!... But they just kept staring ... staring straight ahead. [*He looks at each of them in turn ... silence ... then in a low, broken voice.*] I cannot explain what happened to me then.... My arms ... went limp ... my legs began to tremble ... and a moment later ... it was too late! [*Silence ... he looks at the ground.*] Dora! Was I dreaming ... or did I hear bells ringing?

DORA: No, Yanek, you weren't dreaming. [*She takes his arm.*]

KALIAYEV [*seeing them all looking at him, he raises his head and stands up*]: Yes, look at me ... go on, look at me!... but I'm no coward! I didn't falter, Boria ... I just didn't expect them ... everything happened so quickly ... those two serious little faces and that hideous weight in my hand ... I was going to have to throw it at them ... just like that ... straight at them.... Oh, no!... I just couldn't do it! [*He looks at each of them in turn ... they are all quite still and silent.*] In the old days, when I used to go driving on our estate in the Ukraine, I always drove like a madman, because I wasn't afraid of anything ... except of running down a child. That was my only fear. I used to imagine the shock, the small head hitting the ground.... [*He breaks down*] ... oh, help me ... help me ... [*silence*]. I meant to kill myself just now. I only came back because I thought I owed it to you ... you are the only people who can judge me ... say if I was right or wrong ... but you don't say anything! [*He is desperate ...* DORA *goes to him and touches him.... he looks at them all and then dejectedly ...*] If you decide that those children must die, I shall go to the theatre and wait for them to come out ... I shall throw the bomb and I can promise not to miss ... just make up your minds ... I'll do what you decide.

STEPAN: The Organization ordered you to kill the Grand Duke!

KALIAYEV: Yes, but I wasn't ordered to murder children!

ANNENKOV: Yanek's right – we weren't expecting that.

STEPAN: It was his duty to obey orders.

ANNENKOV: I'm in charge, and I should have foreseen everything so that no one could have hesitated to carry out orders. It was my fault. Now we have to decide if we are to let this chance go by or tell Yanek to wait outside the theatre for them. Alexis?

VOINOV: I don't know what to say.... I think I would have done what Yanek did ... but I'm not sure of myself ... [*more quietly*] It's my hands ... they are trembling.

ANNENKOV: Dora?

DORA [*passionately*]: I would have held back like Yanek. How can I ask others to do what I couldn't do myself?

STEPAN: Do you people realize what this decision means? Two months of shadowing, of hair's-breadth escapes – two wasted months! Egor arrested ... for nothing! Rikov hanged ... for nothing! Have we got to start all over again? Weeks and weeks of endless suspense, of sleepless nights ... plotting and scheming, before we get another opportunity like this. Are you all out of your minds?

ANNENKOV: You know very well that in two days' time the Grand Duke will be going to the theatre again.

STEPAN: Two days ... in which we risk being caught at any moment – you've said so yourself.

KALIAYEV: I'm going...

DORA: No, wait. Stepan, could you fire point blank at a child with your eyes open?

STEPAN: I could if the Organization ordered it.

DORA: Then why did you shut your eyes?

STEPAN: What? I shut my eyes?

DORA: Yes.

STEPAN: Then it was because I wanted to picture the scene more vividly so that my answer could be truthful.

DORA: Open your eyes, Stepan, and try to realize that the Organization would lose its power and its influence, if it tolerated for a moment the idea of children being blown to pieces by our bombs.

STEPAN: I'm sorry, but I don't suffer from a tender heart! Not until the day comes when we stop being sentimental about children, will the revolution triumph and we be masters of the world.

DORA: When that day comes, the revolution will be loathed by the entire human race.

STEPAN: What does that matter if we love it enough to force our revolution on it, to rescue humanity from itself...

DORA: Suppose the whole human race rejects the revolution? Suppose the masses you're fighting for won't put up with their children being killed? Would you strike at *them* too?

STEPAN: Yes, if it was necessary, and I'd go on striking at them until they understood... I too love the people.

DORA: That's not what love is.

STEPAN: Who says it isn't.

DORA: I do.

STEPAN: You are a woman!... and your idea of love is a poor one.

DORA [*violently*]: At least I have a very good idea of what shame is.

STEPAN: Shame? Once and only once in my life have I felt ashamed ... when I was flogged ... yes! *I* was flogged! Do you know what it's like to be flogged. Vera was there beside me... and she killed herself as a protest;

but *I* lived on . . . so why should I be ashamed of anything now?

ANNENKOV: All of us love and respect you, Stepan; but whatever your reasons are for feeling this way, you must not say that anything is justifiable . . . thousands of us have died to prove that everything is *not* justifiable.

STEPAN: Nothing that can serve our cause should be ruled out.

ANNENKOV [*angrily*]: Is it justifiable to go over to the police and play a double game, as Evno suggested?

STEPAN: Yes, if it was necessary.

ANNENKOV [*getting up*]: We will forget what you've said, Stepan, because of all that you have done for us and with us. The point is this: are we or are we not going to throw the bombs at these children?

STEPAN: Children! There you go again, always talking about children! Don't you see what this means? Because Yanek didn't kill those *two, thousands* of Russian children will go on dying of starvation for years to come! Have you ever seen children dying of starvation . . . I have, and to be killed by a bomb is pleasant compared to that . . . but Yanek! . . . Yanek has never seen children starving to death. He only saw the Grand Duke's little pair of lapdogs! Can't you see what will happen, or do you just live for the present? In that case, go on! . . . indulge in charity . . . and cure each petty little suffering that comes along, but don't meddle with the revolution, which exists to cure all suffering . . . now and in the future.

DORA: Yanek will kill the Grand Duke because his death may help to bring nearer the day when Russian children no longer die of starvation. That by itself is no easy task for him, but killing the Grand Duke's niece and nephew won't prevent a single child from starving. Even destruction has a right and a wrong way, and there *are* limits . . .

STEPAN [*violently*]: There are *no* limits ! What it really means is that you don't believe in the revolution ! [*They all get up except* KALIAYEV.] No, you don't believe in it – any of you ! If you had your whole heart in it, if you were sure that our sacrifices and our triumphs will be the foundation of a new Russia, freed from tyranny . . . a land of freedom that will gradually spread over the entire world and if you were convinced that then and only then will man, freed from tyrants and superstitions, at last look up to the sky – a god in his own right, how could the death of two children be weighed in the balance against such a faith ? Surely you'd feel justified in doing anything and everything that might bring that day nearer . . . so, if you won't kill those two children, it simply means that you're not sure you are justified . . . so you don't believe in the revolution ! [*Silence.*]

KALIAYEV [*gets up*]: I am ashamed of myself, Stepan, but I can't let you go on . . . I am ready to kill to overthrow the tyranny, but behind your words I can see the threat of another kind of tyranny . . . and if it ever comes into power, it will make me a murderer ! It's justice that I try to fight for !

STEPAN: What does it matter if you're fighting for justice or you're murderers, as long as justice is done ? You and I, we don't count !

KALIAYEV: Yes, we do and you know it. It's only pride that makes you say that.

STEPAN: My pride is my own business, but man's pride, his rebellions, the injustice that is done to him . . . that concerns us all !

KALIAYEV: Man does not live only by justice . . .

STEPAN: When his bread is stolen, what else has he to live by?

KALIAYEV: By justice . . . and innocence . . .

STEPAN: Innocence? . . . I'm sure I'm aware of it, but I prefer to shut my eyes to it and to shut other men's eyes to it, so that one day it will have a universal meaning.

KALIAYEV: One must be very sure that that day will come, if one denies everything that makes a man willing to live.

STEPAN: I *am* sure it will come.

KALIAYEV: No, you can't be as sure as that! Perhaps as many as three generations will have to be sacrificed before it can be known which of us . . . you or I . . . is right. There will have been many wars and bloody revolutions, and by the time all this blood has seeped into the earth, you and I will long ago have turned to dust!

STEPAN: Then others will come and I will hail them as my brothers.

KALIAYEV [*shouting*]: Others, yes! . . . but I love the men who are alive today . . . who walk on the same earth as I do! It is for *them* that I am fighting, and it is for *them* that I am ready to lay down my life! I shall not strike my brothers in the face for the sake of some unknown . . . distant city! I refuse to add to the living injustice around me for the sake of a . . . dead . . . justice . . . [*more quietly, but firmly*] I want to tell you something that the simplest peasant knows: killing children is a crime against a man's honour, and if the revolution should ever break with honour . . . then I should break with the revolution. If you decide that I must do it, I will go and wait for them to leave the theatre . . . but I will throw myself under the horses' feet.

STEPAN: Honour is a luxury reserved for those who have carriages.

KALIAYEV: No! It is the one wealth left for the poor man. *You* know that, and you know too that the revolution has its honour. It's what we're all prepared to die for! . . . and it's what made you hold up your head, Stepan, when they flogged you and it's behind what you've been saying today.

STEPAN [*with a shout*]: I forbid you to speak of that.

KALIAYEV [*incensed*]: No! . . . I let you tell me that I didn't believe in the revolution, which was as good as telling me that I was prepared to kill the Grand Duke . . . for nothing! . . . that I was nothing but a common murderer! . . . I let you say that and I managed to keep my hands off you . . .

ANNENKOV: Yanek!

STEPAN: Not to kill enough is killing for nothing sometimes.

ANNENKOV: None of us agrees with you, Stepan. We've made up our minds.

STEPAN: Then I accept your . . . decision, but let me tell you again that squeamishness has no place in terrorism. We are murderers and that's what we've chosen to be.

KALIAYEV [*beside himself with rage*]: No! I have chosen death to prevent murder from triumphing in the world . . . I have chosen to be innocent!

ANNENKOV: Yanek! Stepan! That's enough. We've decided that slaughtering these children would serve no purpose. We must start again from the beginning and be ready to try again in two days' time.

STEPAN: And suppose the children are there again?

KALIAYEV: We'll wait for another opportunity.

STEPAN: And if the Grand Duchess is with the Grand Duke?

KALIAYEV: I will not spare her.

ANNENKOV: Listen! [*The sound of a carriage is heard . . .* KALIAYEV *goes irresistibly to the window . . . the others wait*

... the carriage comes nearer, passes by the window and disappears ...]

VOINOV [*looking at* DORA, *who goes towards him*]: Yes, Dora, we will have to start again.

STEPAN [*scornfully*]: Yes, Alexis ... start again; but of course, we must do something for our precious honour ...

CURTAIN

ACT THREE

Scene: The same . . . two days later . . . it is evening.

STEPAN: What's Voinov up to? He should be here by now.

ANNENKOV: He can do with some sleep, and we've got another half hour yet.

STEPAN: I could go down and see if there's any news.

ANNENKOV: No. We mustn't take unnecessary risks. [*Silence.*] Why are you so silent, Yanek?

KALIAYEV: I've got nothing to say, but don't worry about me . . . [*The bell rings once and then twice.*] Here he is!

[*Enter* VOINOV.]

ANNENKOV: Get some sleep?

VOINOV: A bit.

ANNENKOV: Did you sleep all night?

VOINOV: No.

ANNENKOV: You ought to have done. There are ways of making yourself sleep.

VOINOV: I tried . . . but . . . I'm too tired.

ANNENKOV: Your hands are shaking.

VOINOV: No, they're not! [*They are all looking at him.*] Why are you all staring at me? What's wrong with being tired?

ANNENKOV: That's not the point . . . we're concerned about you.

VOINOV [*suddenly violent*]: You should have thought about that two days ago! If the bomb had been thrown then, we wouldn't be tired now.

KALIAYEV: I'm sorry, Alexis. I've made things harder for everyone.

VOINOV [*more quietly*]: What do you mean, harder? I'm tired, that's all.

DORA: Well, it won't be long now ... in an hour it will all be over.

VOINOV: Yes ... it will all be over, in an hour's time ... [*He looks around* ... DORA *gets up and takes his hand* ... *he leaves his hand in hers, then pulls it away.*] Boria, I want to talk to you.

ANNENKOV: In private?

VOINOV: Yes ... in private. [*They all glance at one another* ... KALIAYEV, DORA *and* STEPAN *exit.*]

ANNENKOV: What is it? ... [*Silence.*] Go on ... tell me, Alexis.

VOINOV: I'm ashamed, Boria ... [*Silence.*] I'm ashamed, but I must tell you the truth.

ANNENKOV: You don't want to throw the bomb ... is that it?

VOINOV: I can't bring myself to do it.

ANNENKOV: Do you mean you're scared? Is that it? Is that all? That's nothing to be ashamed of.

VOINOV: Yes, I am scared ... and I *am* ashamed of it.

ANNENKOV: But the day before yesterday you were so happy, so calm. When you went out, there was a gleam in your eye.

VOINOV: I've always been scared. The day before yesterday, I'd summoned up my courage, and when I heard the carriage rumbling in the distance, I said to myself: 'Only a minute to go!' I gritted my teeth ... and every muscle in my body was tense: if I'd thrown the bomb at that moment, I think the force of the throw alone would have killed the Grand Duke. I waited ... waited for the first explosion, which would set everything going . . . and then . . . nothing! It never came! The carriage rumbled past me . . . how fast it went . . . it passed me in a flash . . . and then I realized that Yanek hadn't thrown his bomb. I went cold all over, and suddenly I felt as weak as a child . . .

ANNENKOV: Don't worry, Alexis . . . your strength will return to you.

VOINOV: Two days have gone by, but it hasn't come back. I lied to you just now . . . I could sleep last night. . . . My heart was pounding. Oh, Boria! I give up . . .

ANNENKOV: You mustn't give up, Alexis! We've all been through it as well. You won't be asked to throw the bomb. . . . A month's rest in Finland, and then you can come back to us.

VOINOV: No . . . it's not as simple as that. If I don't throw the bomb today, I'll never throw it.

ANNENKOV: What are you going to do then?

VOINOV: I'll carry on with propaganda and committees, but I wasn't made for terrorism – I realize that now. . . . The best thing is for me to leave you.

ANNENKOV: The risk is the same.

VOINOV: Yes, but you can keep your eyes shut. . . . You don't know . . . and that makes all the difference.

ANNENKOV: What do you mean?

VOINOV [*passionately*]: You don't see what happens; it's easy to go to meetings, to work out plans and then pass on orders to be carried out. You risk your life, I know . . . but there's a sort of veil between you and the real thing: but it's different going down into the street when it's getting dark and standing among the crowds of people hurrying home to their evening meals, their children and their wives waiting on the doorstep . . . and having to stand there ... grim and silent, with the weight of the bomb tugging at your arm ... and knowing that in three minutes, in two minutes, in a few seconds ... you will dash out towards a glistening carriage, the bomb in your hand.... That's what terrorist action is, and I know now that I couldn't start it all over again, without feeling the blood drained from my veins. Yes, I'm ashamed... I aimed too high. I must be given the job I'm fit for – a humble job ... the only one I'm worthy of.

ANNENKOV: There are no humble jobs. All our paths lead to prison and the gallows.

VOINOV: Yes, but they're not staring you in the face. The man you're going to kill ... he's right there in front of you. You have to imagine ... prison and the gallows, and luckily I have no imagination ... [*He laughs nervously.*] I never really did believe in the secret police, you know ... funny, isn't it? ... for a terrorist? I'll believe they exist when I get my first kick in the stomach ... not before.

ANNENKOV: And when you're in prison? You can't help knowing and seeing.... There you have to face facts.

VOINOV: You don't have to make any more decisions in prison! That's what it is ... no more decisions ... no more saying to yourself: 'Now it's up to you, up to *you* to decide when to strike.' One thing I'm sure of now is that I shall not try to escape, if I'm arrested.... You have to make decisions to escape, you have to take the initiative. If you don't try to escape, *they* take the initiative ... they do all the work ...

ANNENKOV: Yes ... they hang you ...

VOINOV: ... but dying will be easier than ... [*desperately*] ... than carrying my life and another's in my hand and having to decide when to plunge those lives into oblivion.... No, Boria, the only way I can redeem myself is to accept myself for what I am ... [*silence*] ... even cowards can help the revolution – they've just got to find out how they can be useful.

ANNENKOV: We are all cowards really, but we aren't always forced to show it.... Well, that's settled then ... it's up to you.

VOINOV: I shall leave at once. I don't think I could face the others. You'll tell them, won't you?

ANNENKOV: Yes ... I'll tell them. [*He goes towards* VOINOV.]

VOINOV: Tell Yanek it's not his fault ... and tell him I love him ... as I love you all ... [*Silence.* ANNENKOV *embraces him.*]

ANNENKOV: Good-bye, Alexis.... It'll work out all right. ... *One* day Russia will be happy!

VOINOV: Oh yes, Boria ... happy! ... happy ... [*They go to the door. Exit* VOINOV.]

ANNENKOV: You can come in now. [*Enter* DORA, STEPAN *and* KALIAYEV.]

STEPAN: What was that about?

ANNENKOV: Voinov isn't going to throw the bomb. He's exhausted and he might bungle it.

KALIAYEV: It's my fault, isn't it, Boria?

ANNENKOV: He asked me to tell you that he loves you.

KALIAYEV: Will we see him again?

ANNENKOV: Maybe.... He's leaving us for the time being.

STEPAN: Why?

ANNENKOV: He'll be more useful on the committees.

STEPAN: Did he ask to go? Has he lost his nerve?

ANNENKOV: No.... It was my decision entirely.

STEPAN: So you're making us one short at the last minute.

ANNENKOV: I had to decide by myself. It was too late to talk it over with you. I shall take Voinov's place...

[STEPAN *makes a gesture of protest and starts to say something.*] No, Stepan.

KALIAYEV: You are our leader, Boria. It's your duty to stay here.

ANNENKOV: Sometimes it is the leader's duty to be a coward, provided that he proves his courage when the time comes. I've made up my mind. Stepan, you will replace me for as long as it is necessary.... Now come and listen to your instructions ... come along. [STEPAN *and* ANNENKOV *exit....* KALIAYEV *sits ...* DORA *goes towards him, her hand outstretched ... but she withdraws it.*]

DORA: It's not your fault, Yanek.

KALIAYEV: I've hurt him ... I've hurt him deeply. Do you know what he said to me the other day?

DORA: He never stopped saying how happy he was.

KALIAYEV: Yes, but he told me that there was no happiness for him, except when he's with us. The Organization is everything in the world today ... and we are the Organization – we are the new spirit of truth. Oh, Dora, why did this have to happen?

DORA: He'll come back.

KALIAYEV: No ... I know what I'd feel like, if I were he, I'd be desperate.

DORA: *Aren't* you desperate?

KALIAYEV [*sadly*]: Now?... now I'm with you, and I'm happy ... as *he* was.

DORA [*slowly*]: Yes, it's a wonderful happiness. [*A pause.*]

KALIAYEV: Yes ... it *is* a wonderful happiness ...

DORA: Then why are you so depressed? Two days ago, your face was shining. You looked as if you were inspired, but today ...

KALIAYEV [*getting up and pacing up and down*]: Today ... today I know something I didn't know then. You were right, Dora – it's not so simple after all. I thought it was easy to kill ... I thought that courage and the ideal would be enough; but I'm not so different, and I now know that there is no happiness in hatred ... I can see the vileness in myself and in the others – murder, cowardice, injustice. ... I've got to kill him ... I've *got* to, but I shall see it through to the end! I shall go beyond hatred!

DORA: Beyond? There is nothing beyond.

KALIAYEV: Yes, there is ... there's love!

DORA: Love? No, that's not what's needed.

KALIAYEV: Dora! How can you say that? ...

DORA: There's too much blood, too much brutality. Those who really have their hearts set on justice have no right to love. They stand upright like me, their heads held high, their eyes fastened on their goal. What room is there for love? Love pulls these proud heads down. ... Our heads must stay high, Yanek.

KALIAYEV: But we love our fellow men!

DORA: Yes, of course we love them, but with a vast, ungrounded love, with an unhappy love. We are so cut off from them, shut in our little rooms, lost in our thoughts ... and do the people love us? ... Do they ever know that we love them? No! The people don't say anything ... not a word.

KALIAYEV: But that's what love is: to give everything, to sacrifice everything, without expecting *anything* in return.

DORA: Perhaps. ... That's what burns in me, an ideal love ... pure lonely joy; yet there are times when I wonder if love is not something else ... something more than just a lonely voice ... I wonder if there isn't some kind of response: I often picture it – the sun shining, heads humbly bowed, hearts no longer proud, arms outstretched. ... Oh, Yanek! If only we could forget, just for an hour, the ugliness of this world, and let ourselves go at last. Just one hour to ourselves! . . . Can you understand that?

KALIAYEV: Yes, Dora . . . I can . . . That's what men call . . . love.

DORA: Oh, you understand everything, darling. Yes, that is love; but does that kind of love mean anything to you? Do you love justice like that? [*Silence.*] Do you love our people with a tender, unselfish love, or with a passion for revolution and revenge? [KALIAYEV *still says nothing.*] You see? [*She goes towards him . . . very quietly and weakly.*] What about *me,* Yanek? Do you love *me*? [*He looks at her in silence.*]

KALIAYEV: No one will ever love you as I do!

DORA: I know . . . but wouldn't it be better to love like other people do?

KALIAYEV: I'm not just other people . . . I love you as I am!

DORA: Yes, but do you love me more than justice, more than the Organization?

KALIAYEV: You, justice and the Organization go together: they are a part of you!

DORA: Yes, but answer me, please answer me! Do you love me with a human love? Do you love me selfishly, possessively? . . . Would you love me if I were unjust?

KALIAYEV: If you were unjust and I could love you. . . . It would not be you that I loved.

DORA: But you're not answering me. Just tell me if you would love me if I were not part of the Organization.

KALIAYEV: Where would you be then?

DORA: I remember when I was at University . . . I was always laughing then. I was quite pretty . . . I used to spend hours wandering around, dreaming. Would you love me if I were like that – carefree and innocent? [*A pause.*]

KALIAYEV [*in a low, desperate voice*]: I'm longing to say yes!

DORA [*with a passionate cry*]: Then *say* yes, darling, if you really mean it ... if it is true ... say yes! Forget justice, and suffering and human slavery.... Please say yes! Forget the scaffold, the writhing children ... men who are whipped to death!...

KALIAYEV: Stop it, Dora!

DORA: No!... For once we must listen to our hearts. I'm waiting for you to tell me that you want me ... *me*, Dora! ... and that I mean more to you than this world ... this foully unjust world!...

KALIAYEV [*brutally*]: Stop it! The only words in my heart ... are of you ... but soon ... I must not flinch!

DORA [*bewildered*]: Soon?... Oh, yes, I'd forgotten ... [*laughing and crying at the same time*] No, it's all right, my love ... Don't be angry ... I was being unreasonable ... I'm just tired ... I couldn't have said it to you either ... I love you in the same way as you love justice and those in prison ... [*A pause.*] Do you remember what summer is like, Yanek?... but no!... it's always winter here. We are not of this world ... we are 'the just' ... There *is* a warmth in the world, but it is not for us... [*Turning away.*] Oh, pity 'the just'!

KALIAYEV [*gazing at her with despair*]: Yes, that's our role here on earth – there's no place for *our* love... [*triumphantly*] ... but I will kill the Grand Duke ... and then there will be peace for both of us!

DORA: Peace! When will we find peace?

KALIAYEV [*violently*]: Tomorrow! [ANNENKOV *and* STEPAN *enter* ... KALIAYEV *and* DORA *move away from one another.*]

ANNENKOV: Yanek!

KALIAYEV: I'm ready. [*Breathes deeply.*] At last! At last!

STEPAN [*going up to him*]: Good-bye, Yanek ... I am with you.

KALIAYEV: Good-bye, Stepan. [*Turns to face* DORA.] Good-bye, Dora ... [*They stand very close to one another but do not touch.*]

DORA: No, not good-bye ... au revoir, au revoir, my love ... we'll meet again ...

KALIAYEV: Au revoir ... [*He gazes at her in silence.*] Dora ... I ... I ... Russia will be a beautiful place!....

DORA [*in tears*]: Yes ... Russia *will* be a beautiful place ...

[KALIAYEV *turns on his heels, crosses himself in front of the prie-dieu and exits with* ANNENKOV ... STEPAN *goes to the window* ... DORA *stands absolutely still, staring at the door.*]

STEPAN: How proudly he's walking. I was wrong not to trust him. I thought his enthusiasm was too romantic. Did you see him cross himself? Does he believe in God?

DORA: Well, he doesn't go to church.

STEPAN: But God is in his soul. That's the difference between us: I am more bitter than he is. For us who don't believe in God, there is nothing between total justice and utter despair.

DORA: For Yanek, there is despair even in justice.

STEPAN: Yes, he has a weak soul ... but a strong hand; he will kill him ... I know he will ... and that's the main thing: we must destroy ... but you say nothing. [*He looks at her intently.*] Do you love him? [*A pause.*]

DORA: We need time for love.... We scarcely have time for justice.

STEPAN: You're right: there's too much to do. We must blow this world to pieces, and after that ... [*at the window*]. They're out of sight ... they must be there.

DORA: And after that?

STEPAN: We shall love one another.

DORA: If we're still alive.

STEPAN: Then other people will love each other, which is the same thing. [*A pause.*]

DORA: Stepan, say 'hate'.

STEPAN: What?

DORA: I just want to hear you say that word ... 'hate'.

STEPAN: Hate.

DORA: Yes, that's right ... Yanek could never say it well.

STEPAN [*after a short silence, coming towards her*]: I see ... you despise me ... Are you sure you're right though? [*Pauses and then continues with rising passion.*] You're all the same, grudging what you do in the name of your despicable love! ... *I* don't love anything ... I *hate*, yes I hate, my fellow men. Why should I want their precious love? I knew that three years ago in prison. ... Three years I've borne its marks on me ... and you want me to turn sentimental and carry the bomb like a cross! Oh, no! I've seen too much! Look! ... [*He tears his shirt open ...* DORA, *horrified, shrinks away at the sight of lashmarks on his back.*] There you are! There are the marks of their love! Now ... do you still despise me? [*She quickly embraces him.*]

DORA: Who could despise suffering? I love you too.

STEPAN [*he looks at her ... murmuring*]: I'm sorry, Dora. [*A pause ... he turns away.*] Perhaps I'm just worn out. All those years of struggling and suspense, of police-spies and prisons, and finally ... [*points to the scars*] ... this. How could I have the strength to love? At least I've got the strength to hate ... that's better than feeling nothing.

DORA: Yes, it is better. [*He looks at her ... seven o'clock strikes in the distance.*]

STEPAN [*swinging round*]: The Duke will be going by ... [DORA *runs to the window and presses her forehead against it ... a long silence ... then in the distance a carriage can be heard ... it draws nearer and then goes by the window.*] Let's hope he's alone! [*The noise of the carriage grows fainter . . . then a violent explosion . . .* DORA *starts violently and buries her head in her hands. A long silence.*] Boria hasn't thrown his bomb . . . Yanek has done it! The people have triumphed!

DORA [*in tears, she flings herself against* STEPAN]: It's *we* who have killed him . . . it's *we* who have killed him! *I* have killed him!

STEPAN [*with a shout*]: Who have we killed? Yanek?

DORA: The Duke!

CURTAIN

ACT FOUR

Scene: A cell in the Pougatchev Tower, Boutirki prison. It is morning. When the curtain rises, KALIAYEV *is in his cell, staring at the door. Enter a guard shoving a prisoner, who is carrying a bucket.*

GUARD: Get on with it. [*He stands by the window....* FOKA, *the prisoner, begins to clean without looking at* KALIAYEV... *silence.*]

KALIAYEV: What's your name, friend?

FOKA: Foka.

KALIAYEV: Are you a prisoner?

FOKA: Looks like it.

KALIAYEV: What did you do?

FOKA: I killed a few people.

KALIAYEV: Were you hungry?

GUARD: Keep it quiet.

KALIAYEV: What?

GUARD: I said keep it quiet! You're not really meant to talk – so keep your voice down like 'im.

KALIAYEV: Were you hungry?

FOKA: No, I was thirsty.

KALIAYEV: What happened?

FOKA: Well ... there was this hatchet lying around, and I really laid about with it good and proper: I killed three people, so they tell me. [KALIAYEV *looks at* FOKA.] Aah, my young gentleman, I see you aren't calling me friend any more. Gone all 'aughty, eh?

KALIAYEV: No ... I killed someone as well.

FOKA: How many?

KALIAYEV: I'll tell you if you like, my friend . . . but, tell me, you regret what you did now, don't you?

FOKA: Gawd! Do I regret it? Huh . . . twenty years, it's a long time . . . enough to make anyone regret it.

KALIAYEV: Twenty years! I come here when I'm twenty-three . . . I'd be an old man by the time I got out.

FOKA: Well, it probably won't be so bad for you. You never can tell with these judges; depends whether he's married and what his wife's like . . . and anyway, you're a gentleman, and it ain't the same for you gentlemen and us poor buggers. You'll get away with it.

KALIAYEV: I doubt it . . . I don't want to get away with it anyway: being ashamed for twenty years . . . I couldn't stand it.

FOKA: What yer mean, ashamed? That's just the sort of thing a gentleman like you would say. . . . How many people did you kill?

KALIAYEV: Only one.

FOKA: Only one? Well . . . that's nothing.

KALIAYEV: I killed the Grand Duke.

FOKA: The Grand Duke, eh? Go on! Typical of you gentlemen. . . . You're really in trouble then, aren't you?

KALIAYEV: Yes . . . but I had to do it.

FOKA: Why? You lived at Court, didn't you? A woman, eh? Was that it? Yeh . . . a good-looking young lad like you . . .

KALIAYEV: I'm a socialist.

GUARD: Not so loud!

KALIAYEV [*louder*]: I'm a revolutionary socialist!

FOKA: That's a good one! Why the hell did you have to go and be a like you say? All you had to do was to stay put and you'd've been well away. The world was made for you gentlemen.

KALIAYEV: No! . . . the world was made for you, my friend. Oh, there are too many crimes, too much poverty in the world today. One day, when there's less poverty there'll be fewer crimes. If Russia were free, you would not be here.

FOKA: Yes, well . . . one thing's certain, whether you're free or not – it's not worth having one too many.

KALIAYEV: There's never any point. Usually a man only takes to drink because he's oppressed. A day will come when there'll be no point in drinking, when nobody will be ashamed . . . neither gentleman, nor poor peasant; we'll all be brothers . . . and justice will make our hearts pure and innocent . . . [*A pause.*] Do you understand what I'm saying?

FOKA: Yeh, you mean the kingdom of God.

GUARD: Keep your voices down!

KALIAYEV: No, it's not that! . . . God can do nothing! Justice is our concern. [*Silence.*] Don't you understand? Do you know the story of St Dmitri?

FOKA: No.

KALIAYEV: Well, he'd made an appointment with God, far out on the Steppes, and on the way he met a peasant whose cart was stuck in the mud; so St Dmitri stopped to help him. The wheels had sunk so far into the mud that it took him an hour to pull the cart out. When he had done it, St Dmitri ran on to keep his appointment . . . but when he got there . . . God had gone.

FOKA: So?

KALIAYEV: Well, there are always some who arrive too late, because there are too many carts stuck in the mud . . . too many others who need help. [FOKA *recoils uneasily.*] What's wrong?

GUARD: Not so loud . . . and you! . . . get on with it.

FOKA: It ain't natural . . . all this stuff about saints and carts and whatnot. Seems bloody silly getting put in prison for ideas like that. . . . Yes, and there's another thing . . . [*The* GUARD *laughs.*]

KALIAYEV [*looking at him*]: What?

FOKA: What happens to people who kill Grand Dukes?

KALIAYEV: They hang.

FOKA: Yes, they do . . . [*He makes his way out . . . the* GUARD *laughs louder.*]

KALIAYEV: Wait? What have I done?

FOKA: You ain't done nothing. . . . It's just that I wouldn't like to make a fool of a fine gentleman like you. I mean, it's all right talking like that just to pass the time, but . . . but if you're going to be hanged . . . well, I mean, well . . . it just ain't fair.

KALIAYEV: Why?

GUARD [*still laughing*]: Go on, then . . . tell him.

FOKA: Well, all this talk about you and me being brothers, isn't any use . . . I'm the hangman . . .

KALIAYEV: I thought you were a prisoner like me.

FOKA: Yes, I am, but they've given me the job of hangman as well . . . I get a year knocked off my sentence for each one I hang . . . suits me.

KALIAYEV: So, to pay for your crimes . . . they make you commit new ones.

FOKA: No, they're not crimes . . . I'm just carrying out orders. Anyway, they don't care: it's all the same to them: if you ask me, they're not Christians.

KALIAYEV: How many people have you . . . hanged . . . so far?

FOKA: Two. [KALIAYEV *winces.* FOKA *and the* GUARD *reach the door . . . the* GUARD *gives* FOKA *a shove.*]

KALIAYEV: So you're an executioner, are you?

FOKA [*from the doorway*]: And you, sir . . . what about you?

[FOKA *and the* GUARD *exit ... noise of footsteps and orders can be heard ... enter* SKOURATOV, *Chief of Police, followed by the* GUARD ... SKOURATOV *is very elegant.*]

SKOURATOV [*to the* GUARD]: You can go now. Good morning. You don't know me, do you? I know *you*, though ... [*he laughs*] ... famous already, eh? [*He looks at* KALIAYEV.] May I introduce myself? [KALIAYEV *says nothing.*] Oh, you don't feel like talking. I quite understand. A week in solitary confinement ... wears a man down, eh? Well, we've put a stop to that: from now on you can have visitors; in fact, I've sent you one already – old Foka ... curious fellow, isn't he? I thought you'd find him interesting. You must be pleased with the change; it's good to see a human face again, after a week's solitary confinement ... isn't it?

KALIAYEV: It depends on the face.

SKOURATOV: Aha, quite ... I see you know your own mind. Unless I'm very much mistaken, my face displeases you.

KALIAYEV: Yes.

SKOURATOV: You disappoint me ... still I have hopes that you may change your mind. For one thing, the lighting's bad; these basement cells make everyone look ghastly ... and, of course, you don't know me. Sometimes a man's face puts one off at first, and then later, when one gets to know the man himself ...

KALIAYEV: Who are you?

SKOURATOV: Skouratov, Chief of Police.

KALIAYEV: A lackey.

SKOURATOV: At your service, but if I were in your position, I wouldn't be too sure of myself ... I wouldn't throw my weight around, but you'll learn. You begin by wanting justice, and in the end you set up a police force. Anyway, the truth doesn't frighten me, I'm going to be frank with you. . . . You interest me; I'm going to offer you a pardon.

KALIAYEV: What do you mean?

SKOURATOV: I should have thought it was obvious – I'm offering you your life.

KALIAYEV: Who asked you for it?

SKOURATOV: One does not ask for life, my young friend; one is given it. Haven't you ever let anyone off? [*A pause.*] Think hard . . .

KALIAYEV: I do not want your pardon . . . and that's all there is to it.

SKOURATOV: Well, at least listen to me. I'm not your enemy, even if I seem to be. I won't even say that your ideas are wrong . . . except when they lead to murder . . .

KALIAYEV: Do not use that word!

SKOURATOV [*looking at him*]: Aha, you *are* on edge, aren't you? [*a pause*] . . . but no, really, I want to help you.

KALIAYEV: Help me? . . . I'm ready to pay for what I've done, but I don't want you and your . . . friendliness! Get out.

SKOURATOV: The charge you have to face . . .

KALIAYEV: There is no charge! I'm a prisoner of war . . . not a criminal.

SKOURATOV: Very well, but harm has been done, has it not? Let's leave politics out of it: a man has been killed, and in a particularly horrible manner.

KALIAYEV: I threw the bomb at your tyranny, not at a man!

SKOURATOV: No doubt, but you still killed a man, and it wasn't a pretty sight, my friend. When they had recovered the body, the head was missing . . . completely disappeared! The only things that could be recognized were an arm and a bit of a leg.

KALIAYEV: I have carried out a sentence.

SKOURATOV: Perhaps, but . . . no one is blaming you for the sentence; what is a sentence, anyway? It's just a word . . . a word you can argue about for days. What you're accused of . . . of course, you don't like that word . . . is a sort of amateur job, a messy one in fact. The results – they're plain enough to see, there's no disputing *them.* Ask the Grand Duchess. . . . There was blood, you know . . . a lot of blood . . .

KALIAYEV: Be quiet!

SKOURATOV [*his tone changes*]: All right, but I just want to say that if you persist in talking about a sentence, and insist that it was the party and the party alone that tried and condemned the Grand Duke to death, in fact that he was killed not by a bomb but by an idea, then you don't need a pardon . . . but suppose we get back to the facts! Suppose we say that it was you, Ivan Kaliayev, who blew the Grand Duke's head to pieces . . . that's a different matter altogether, isn't it? You'll need to be pardoned *then*; and that's how I want to help you . . . purely out of the kindness of my heart, I assure you. [*He smiles.*] What else can you expect from me? I'm not interested in ideas, I'm interested in people.

KALIAYEV [*exploding*]: You and your employers have got no power over me! You can kill me, but you cannot pass judgement on me! Oh, I know what you're getting at: you're trying to find a chink in my armour, you're hoping to make me feel ashamed of myself and burst into tears, and repent of what you call my crime! . . . Well, you won't get anywhere. What I am is nothing to do with you. What concerns you is our hatred . . . mine and my brothers! . . . and you're welcome to it!

SKOURATOV: Hatred? That too is just an idea . . . but

murder ... is more than just an idea – it has its repercussions: I mean, of course, repentance and punishment, and that is the point; in fact, that is why I joined the police – to be at the heart of things ... but you don't want to hear me talking about myself. [*A pause ... he goes slowly towards him.*] What I'm getting at is, you shouldn't pretend to forget the Grand Duke's head. If you keep this in mind, you'd find that a mere ideal is not enough. To start with, you'd be ashamed of what you've done, not proud of it; and as soon as you felt ashamed, you'd want to live to redeem yourself. The most important thing, therefore, is that you make up your mind to live.

KALIAYEV: And if I do?

SKOURATOV: Pardon ... for you and your friends.

KALIAYEV: Have you arrested them?

SKOURATOV: No ... not yet; but if you decide to live, we *shall* arrest them.

KALIAYEV: I'm not sure that I understand you ...

SKOURATOV: I'm sure you *do*. Don't lose your temper yet; think it over first. Your ideal cannot allow you to hand them over to us, but from a practical point of view you'd be doing them a service: you would be saving them from further trouble, and at the same time you would save them from ... the gallows, but, above all, you'd find peace of mind. So, whichever way you look at it, it's the best thing for you to do ... [*A pause.*] Well?

KALIAYEV: You'll find out the answer before long ... from my brothers.

SKOURATOV: Another crime? It seems to be quite a vocation. Well, I've had my say, and I must confess that I'm disappointed; I see that you still cling to your ideal – I can't tear you away from it.

KALIAYEV: You cannot tear me from my brothers!

SKOURATOV: Good-bye, then. [*He is about to go out, then turns round again.*] Why did you spare the Grand Duchess and her niece and nephew?

KALIAYEV: Who told you that?

SKOURATOV: Your informer – he was giving us a bit of information too ... but why did you spare them?

KALIAYEV: It's nothing to do with you!

SKOURATOV [*laughing*]: You think not, eh? Well, I'll tell you why you spared them.... An ideal can kill the Grand Duke, but when it comes to killing children, it's a different matter–you found that out yourself ... but let's carry it a stage further: if an ideal does not justify the killing of children, does it in fact justify the killing ... of the Grand Duke? [KALIAYEV *makes a sign of defiance.*] No, don't answer *me* ... give your answer to the Grand Duchess.

KALIAYEV: The Grand Duchess?

SKOURATOV: Yes, she wants to see you, and the main reason for my coming here was to make it possible for her to speak to you ... which she will do in a minute. She might even make you change your mind; the Grand Duchess is a Christian ... in fact, she's an expert ... on the soul. [*He laughs.*]

KALIAYEV: I refuse to see her!

SKOURATOV: I'm sorry, but she insists on seeing you. After all, you owe her some consideration. What is more, since her husband's death, I am told she has become... mentally unbalanced, so we didn't want to stand in her way. [*He is at the door.*] If you *do* change your mind, don't forget my offer: I'll be seeing you again. [*A pause ... he listens.*] She's coming now. First the police ... and now ... religion! You *are* being spoilt, aren't you? But everything holds together. Imagine God without prisons!... What solitude! [*Exit* SKOURATOV ... *voices and words of command ring out ... enter the* GRAND DUCHESS ... *she stands quite still ... she does not speak ... the door is open.*]

KALIAYEV: What do you want?

GRAND DUCHESS [*uncovering her face*]: Look ... [KALIAYEV *says nothing.*] Many things die with a man ...

KALIAYEV: I realized that.

GRAND DUCHESS: No.... Murderers do not know that; if they did, how could they kill? [*She speaks naturally, but her voice is strained ... a pause.*]

KALIAYEV: I have seen you ... and now I want to be alone.

GRAND DUCHESS: No, I must look at you. [*He recoils ... she sits ... she seems worn out ...*] I can't stay by myself any longer.... Before, when I was miserable, he used to share my sorrow ... I didn't mind suffering then, but now.... No, I can't bear it any longer.... Loneliness ... silence ... but whom can I talk to? The others don't know what it's like. They pretend to be distressed! ... and they really are ... for an hour or so; then they go off to eat ... or sleep – yes, sleep. I thought that you must be like me.... You don't sleep, do you? Whom could I speak to about the crime except to the murderer?

KALIAYEV: What crime? I remember only an act of justice.

GRAND DUCHESS: The same voice! Your voice is exactly like his; but then all men sound the same when they speak of justice.... He used to say: 'That is just', and nobody could question it, and yet ... perhaps he was wrong ... perhaps you are wrong too ...

KALIAYEV: He was the living, human symbol of the supreme injustice which the Russian people have suffered for centuries! In return for that ... he received only privileges! But I ... even if I am wrong ... *my* wages are prison and death ...

GRAND DUCHESS: I know that you are suffering, but what about him? You killed him!

KALIAYEV: He died suddenly.... A death like that is nothing.

GRAND DUCHESS: Nothing!... [*quieter*]. Yes, I suppose so. They took you away immediately. They tell me you made speeches while you were surrounded by the police; yes... that must have helped you ... but I ... I arrived a few minutes later, and I saw it all ... I picked up what I could ... all that blood ... [*A pause.*] I was wearing a white dress...

KALIAYEV: Stop!

GRAND DUCHESS: Why? It's only the truth! Do you know what he was doing two hours before he died? He was sleeping... in an armchair, with his feet up – he often used to do that.... He was sleeping ... and *you* ... you were waiting for him in the ... cruel twilight.... Oh, please help me; you are young, you cannot be wicked. [*She is in tears* ... KALIAYEV *recoils and stiffens.*]

KALIAYEV: I never had time ... to be young.

GRAND DUCHESS: Why do you stiffen like that? Have you never felt sorry for yourself?

KALIAYEV: No.

GRAND DUCHESS: You are wrong – it comforts you. I no longer pity anyone but myself... [*A pause.*] I am ill.... You should have killed me with him, instead of sparing me.

KALIAYEV: I didn't spare *you* ... I spared the children you had with you.

GRAND DUCHESS: Yes... I know. I didn't like them much. They are the Grand Duke's niece and nephew – aren't they as guilty as their uncle?

KALIAYEV: No!

GRAND DUCHESS: Do you know them? My niece is a heartless little girl; she always refuses to give anything to the poor when she's asked to. She won't go near them. Isn't *she* unjust? Of course she is! But he ... he used to love the peasants ... he used to drink with them ... and you killed him. You're unjust as well! The world is empty and cruel ...

KALIAYEV: You're wasting your time. You're just trying to wear me down and make me give in.... Well, you won't do it, so leave me alone.

GRAND DUCHESS: Won't you pray with me and repent? We wouldn't be so lonely then.

KALIAYEV: Let me prepare for death.... If I didn't die, then I *would* be a murderer!

GRAND DUCHESS [*she stands up*]: Die? You really want to die? No! [*She goes towards him ... she is very worried.*] You must live ... and face up to being a murderer. After all, you did kill him, didn't you. Only God can justify you.

KALIAYEV: What God? Yours ... or mine?

GRAND DUCHESS: The God of the Holy Church.

KALIAYEV: The Church has got nothing to do with it!

GRAND DUCHESS: The Church serves a master, who was imprisoned ... just like you.

KALIAYEV: Times have changed: the Church has just chosen what it wants from its master's suffering.

GRAND DUCHESS: What do you mean, chosen?

KALIAYEV: The Church has kept grace for itself ... and it's left us to exercise charity!

GRAND DUCHESS: Whom do you mean by us?

KALIAYEV [*shouting*]: All those you hang! [*Silence.*]

GRAND DUCHESS [*gently*]: I'm not your enemy.

KALIAYEV [*he is desperate*]: Yes you are! You are! ... and so are all the rest of you! There's something even fouler than *being* a criminal, and that is forcing a man into crime who wasn't made for it.... Look at me ... I swear to you I wasn't born a murderer.

GRAND DUCHESS: Don't talk to me as if I were your enemy ... [*She closes the door.*] Look! I'm at your mercy ... we are separated by blood, but we can be united in God ... in a common tragedy. Please, just pray with me ... [*She is crying.*]

KALIAYEV: No! [*He goes towards her.*] I feel only pity for you ... and you have touched my heart – and now I'll hide nothing from you ... I want you to understand: I no longer expect to see God, but when I die, I shall keep the promise I made to those I love ... my brothers, who will be thinking of me at this moment.... If I were to pray now ... I would betray them!

GRAND DUCHESS: What do you mean?

KALIAYEV [*triumphantly*]: Nothing ... except that soon ... I shall be happy! A long ordeal lies ahead for me, but I shall see it through ... and then ... when they've pronounced the sentence, and they're all ready for the execution ... then ... at the foot of the scaffold ... I shall turn away from you and this vile world. [*Quieter and in an intense whisper.*] And at last my heart will be filled with love!... Can you understand?

GRAND DUCHESS: There is no love except with God.

KALIAYEV: Yes, there is.... Love for people ... love for mankind!

GRAND DUCHESS: But men are vile.... You can either forgive them or destroy them. What else can you do?

KALIAYEV: You can ... die with them!

GRAND DUCHESS: But you die alone.... *He* died alone.

KALIAYEV [*desperately*]: No ... no, you *can* die with them. Those who love one another today must die together if they are to be re-united. In life ... they are cut off by injustice, sorrow, shame ... by the evil that men do to one another, by crime. ... Living is agony ... because living is separation!

GRAND DUCHESS: God reunites us.

KALIAYEV: But not on this earth, and it is this earth that counts!

GRAND DUCHESS: This is a world full of dogs, their noses fixed to the ground, sniffing everywhere ... but they never find what they want.

KALIAYEV: Soon I shall know! ... [*a pause*] ... and yet ... can't you imagine a love ... a love between two people, who have given up all hope of joy and who love each other in sorrow ... two people whose only link ... is sorrow! [*He looks at her.*] Can't you imagine that same bond uniting them in death as well?

GRAND DUCHESS: What is this terrible love?

KALIAYEV: The only kind of love that you and the rest of you have ever allowed us!

GRAND DUCHESS: I too loved. The man you killed ...

KALIAYEV: I know. ... That is why I forgive you for the wrong you have done me. [*A pause.*] Now please go. [*A long silence.*]

GRAND DUCHESS [*getting up*]: Yes, I shall go now. I came here to bring you back to God. I realize that now. But you wish to be your own judge and save yourself alone. That is beyond your power ... but God can do it, if you live; I will ask that you be granted a pardon.

KALIAYEV: No, no! ... Don't do that ... please! Let me die, or I shall hate you mortally.

GRAND DUCHESS [*at the door*]: I shall ask your pardon ... from man and from God.

KALIAYEV: No! You can't do that! [*The* GRAND DUCHESS

exits ... KALIAYEV *runs to the door* ... SKOURATOV suddenly appears ... KALIAYEV *starts, closes his eyes, then looks at* SKOURATOV *again.*] Thank God you're here!

SKOURATOV: Delighted.... Why?

KALIAYEV: Because I need someone ... to despise again.

SKOURATOV: Oh, that's a pity.... Well, I have come for your answer.

KALIAYEV: You've had my answer already.

SKOURATOV [*changing his tone*]: No, not yet I haven't! Now just you listen. I arranged this meeting between you and the Grand Duchess so that I could put an account of it in the papers tomorrow. The report will be perfectly correct except on one point.... It will contain a statement saying that you have repented of your crime. Your friends will think that you have betrayed them!

KALIAYEV [*calmly*]: They will not believe it.

SKOURATOV: I shall withdraw this statement only if you make a full confession – you have got all night to make up your mind. [*He turns to the doorway.*]

KALIAYEV [*louder*]: They will not believe it!

SKOURATOV [*turning round*]: Why not? Have they never faltered? [*A pause.*]

KALIAYEV: You do not know ... their love!

SKOURATOV: No, but I know that a man cannot believe in 'brotherhood' for a whole night ... without a single moment of doubt.... So, I shall wait for that moment. [*He closes the door, his back pressed against it.*] Take your time, my friend ... I'm very patient. [*They stand face to face, quite still....*]

CURTAIN

ACT FIVE

Scene: Another flat, similar in style. . . . A week later. It is midnight. Silence . . . DORA *is walking up and down.*

ANNENKOV: You must try to relax, Dora.

DORA: I'm cold.

ANNENKOV: Come and lie down here . . . cover yourself up.

DORA [*still walking up and down*]: How the night drags . . . I'm so cold, Boria. [*There is a knock on the door, then two knocks . . .* ANNENKOV *gets up and goes to open the door . . .* STEPAN *and* VOINOV *enter . . .* VOINOV *goes to* DORA *and embraces her. She presses him close to her.*] Oh, Alexis!

STEPAN: Orlov says that it may be tonight. All the junior officers who aren't on duty have been told to report to the prison. That'll be the excuse for him being there.

ANNENKOV: Where are you going to meet him?

STEPAN: He's going to wait for Voinov and me at the restaurant in Sophiskaia Street.

DORA: So, it's tonight, Boria . . . [*She sits . . . exhausted.*]

ANNENKOV: There's still a chance. The decision rests with the Tsar.

STEPAN: Yes . . . the decision will rest with the Tsar, if Yanek has asked for a pardon.

DORA: He hasn't.

STEPAN: Why should he see the Grand Duchess if he didn't want a pardon? Besides, she says that he repented. How can we be sure?

DORA: We know what he said at the trial and what he said in his letter. Didn't he say that his only regret was that he didn't have *another* life to hurl in the face of tyranny? Could the man who said that beg for a pardon, or repent? No! . . . He wanted to die, and he still does. There's no going back on what he's done.

STEPAN: He shouldn't have seen the Grand Duchess.

DORA: He was the judge of that.

STEPAN: No . . . it was against our principles that he saw her.

DORA: Our only principle is to kill. Now at last he's free . . . Quite free!

STEPAN: No, not yet.

DORA: He is, he is! And now that he is so close to death, he has a right to do what he wants. Yes, he *will* die . . . you won't be disappointed.

ANNENKOV: Dora! . . .

DORA: Yes, you'd be pleased if he was pardoned! It would prove that the Grand Duchess was telling the truth, wouldn't it? He would have repented . . . he would have betrayed us; but if he dies, you will believe in him, and you can still love him . . . [*She looks at them.*] Your love demands a lot.

VOINOV [*going towards her*]: No, Dora, you're wrong. We never doubted him.

DORA [*pacing up and down*]: Didn't you? . . . No, perhaps not, I'm sorry. But anyway what does it matter, we'll know for certain tonight. Oh, Alexis, what did you come back for?

VOINOV: To replace him. I was so proud when I read what he said at the trial; I cried. You remember what he said: 'Death will be my supreme protest against a world of blood and tears.' . . . My hands shook when I read that.

DORA: 'A world of blood and tears.'... Yes he said that, didn't he?

VOINOV: Oh, Dora, what courage. And then his last great cry: 'If I have proved equal to man's protest against violence in the world, then may death crown my work by the purity of the ideal.' That was when I decided to come back.

DORA [*her head in her hands*]: Yes ... he always longed for purity, but oh, what a cruel fulfilment!

VOINOV: Don't cry, Dora. He asked that nobody should cry when he died. Oh, I understand him so well now; I couldn't mistrust him. I suffered because I was a coward, then I threw the bomb at Tiflis, and now I'm no different from Yanek. When I heard that he'd been sentenced to death, the only thing I could think of was taking his place ... as I wasn't able to be beside him.

DORA: Who can take his place tonight? He will be alone, Alexis.

VOINOV: We must support him with our pride, as he supports us with his example. Don't cry.

DORA: Look. ... My eyes are dry, but proud. ... Oh, no ... I can never be proud again!

STEPAN: Don't judge me too harshly, Dora; I would like Yanek to live. We need men like him.

DORA: But he doesn't want to live! ... and so we must want him to die too.

ANNENKOV: You're mad.

DORA: We must ... I know him. That's the only way he'll find peace ... in death. So let him die ... [*softer*] but quickly ...

STEPAN: I'm off, Boria. Come on, Alexis – Orlov is waiting for us.

ANNENKOV: Yes, you'd better go. Hurry back. [STEPAN *amd* VOINOV *go to the door* ... STEPAN *turns and looks at* DORA.]

STEPAN: In a few minutes we shall know everything.... Look after her, Boria. [*Exit* STEPAN *and* VOINOV ... DORA *goes to the window, watched by* ANNENKOV.]

DORA: Death! The gallows! Oh, Boria, it's always death!

ANNENKOV: Yes, Dora ... but there's no other way.

DORA: Don't say that! If death is the only way, then we have chosen the wrong path. The right path leads to life ... a life where the sun shines. You can't be cold all the time ...

ANNENKOV: Our path leads to life as well. Life for others ... Russia will live, our grandchildren will *live*. Do you remember what Yanek used to say? 'Russia will be beautiful.'

DORA: Others ... our grandchildren ... yes, but Yanek is in prison and the rope is cold.... He is going to die ... perhaps he's dead already ... dead so that others may live. But, Boria, suppose the others don't live! Suppose he's dying for nothing!

ANNENKOV: Be quiet! [*Silence.*]

DORA: It's so cold ... but the spring is here.... There are trees in the prison yard ... I know there are. He must see them ...

ANNENKOV: Wait until we know, Dora ... and try to stop shivering.

DORA: I'm so cold ... I feel as though I'm dead already. [*A pause.*] I feel so old: we shall never be young again, Boria. We lose sight of childhood at the first murder; I throw the bomb and then in one second a whole lifetime goes by, and all that remains ... is death: we have gone through one age of man.

ANNENKOV: Then we must go down fighting like men.

DORA: We've gone too fast ... we're no longer men.

ANNENKOV: Misery and injustice also move fast. There's

no time for patience any more, no time to mature gradually. Russia is in a hurry.

DORA: I know. We bear the world's suffering. He did it too. . . . It takes great courage . . . but sometimes I wonder if we will be punished for our pride.

ANNENKOV: It's a pride that we pay for with our lives. No one can go further; we have a right to it.

DORA: Can we be sure that no one will go any further? Sometimes when I listen to Stepan, I'm afraid: perhaps others will come and justify themselves by our example and not pay with their lives!

ANNENKOV: Then they would be cowards.

DORA: Who knows? Perhaps that's what justice is. . . . Then no one would dare look justice in the face again.

ANNENKOV: Dora! [*Silence.*] Are you losing faith? You've never been like this before.

DORA: I'm so cold. I keep thinking how he must not shiver, in case he seems to be afraid.

ANNENKOV: Aren't you with us any more, Dora?

DORA [*throwing herself into his arms*]: Oh, Boria, of course I am! I'm with you to the end. I hate tyranny and I know that this is the only way . . . but when I chose it I was happy . . . not any more: that's the difference. . . . We are prisoners.

ANNENKOV: The whole of Russia is in chains, but we will break them.

DORA: Just give me the bomb and you'll see; I shall walk straight into the flames and I shall not flinch. . . . Oh, it's so much easier to die with one's conflicts than to live with them! [*A pause.*] Boria? . . . have you ever been in love?

ANNENKOV: Yes . . . but it was so long ago, I can't really remember.

DORA: How long ago?

ANNENKOV: Four years.

DORA: How long have you been leader of the Organization?

ANNENKOV: Four years. [*A pause.*] Now it's the Organization I love.

DORA [*going towards the window*]: To love, yes ... but to *be* loved, no! ... no, we must keep going, keep going on and on. If only we could pause just for a little while. No, go on, keep on.... If only we could hold out our arms and be ourselves! ... but vile injustice clings to us like a leech – keep on! We are condemned to be greater than ourselves. People, faces ... they are what we'd like to love: love instead of justice! No, we must go on ... [*She is in tears.*] Keep going ... Dora ... keep ... going ... Yanek.... But the end is coming for him ...

ANNENKOV [*taking her in his arms*]: He'll get a pardon.

DORA [*looking at him*]: You know that he won't.... You know that he musn't! [*He looks away.*] Perhaps he's already standing in the prison yard.... There is a sudden hush when he appears. As long as he isn't cold ... Boria! Do you know how they hang people?

ANNENKOV: No, Dora!

DORA [*wildly*]: The hangman jumps on to your shoulders and your neck ... cracks! [*A pause ... with a shriek.*] Isn't it ghastly?

ANNENKOV: Yes, in a way ... and in another way it's rather wonderful.

DORA: Wonderful?

ANNENKOV: Yes ... to feel a man's hand just before you die. [DORA *turns and throws herself into a chair ... silence.*] You must go away and have a rest as soon as it's all over, Dora.

DORA [*distraught*]: Go away? Who with?

ANNENKOV: With me, Dora.

DORA [*she looks at him*]: Go away? . . . [*Turns to the window.*] Ah, it's morning: Yanek's dead already! . . . I can feel it. [*Silence.*]

ANNENKOV: I am your brother.

DORA: Yes . . . you're my brother, you're all my brothers, my brothers whom I love . . . but what a foul taste brotherhood sometimes has! [*It is raining . . . day is breaking . . . there is a knock at the door, followed by two more . . .* STEPAN *and* VOINOV *enter . . . no one moves . . .* DORA *staggers, but recovers herself.*]

STEPAN: [*A pause . . . in a low voice.*] Yanek . . . hasn't betrayed us.

ANNENKOV: Did Orlov see what happened?

STEPAN: Yes.

DORA [*going steadily towards* STEPAN]: Sit down, Stepan. . . . Tell me what happened.

STEPAN: What's the use?

DORA: Tell me everything; I have a right to know. . . . You've got to tell me . . . every detail . . .

STEPAN: I can't tell you. Anyway we've got to leave now.

DORA: No, you must tell me first. When was he told?

STEPAN: Ten o'clock last night.

DORA: When did they hang him?

STEPAN: Two o'clock this morning.

DORA: So he waited in his cell for four hours . . .

STEPAN: Yes . . . without a word. Then suddenly everything happened; and now it's all over.

DORA: Four hours without speaking. What was he wearing? Did he have on his fur-lined coat?

STEPAN: No. He had a black suit on, and his black felt hat, but he wasn't wearing a coat.

DORA: Was it cold?

STEPAN: Well, it was pitch dark . . . and there was snow on the ground . . . then the rain came and turned it to slush.

DORA [*looking at him intently*]: Was he shivering?

STEPAN: No.

DORA: Did Orlov catch his eye?

STEPAN: No.

DORA: Who was he looking at?

STEPAN: Orlov says he was looking at everyone . . . but he didn't seem to see anyone.

DORA: And then? What happened next?

STEPAN: That's enough, Dora.

DORA: No! I want to know; his death belongs to me, if nothing else does!

STEPAN: They read the verdict.

DORA: What did he do while it was being read?

STEPAN: Nothing . . . but just once, he shook his leg to get rid of a bit of mud stuck to his shoe.

DORA [*her head in her hands*]: A bit of mud!

ANNENKOV [*sharply*]: How do you know all this? You asked Orlov to tell you every detail . . . why? [STEPAN *says nothing.*]

STEPAN [*quietly . . . looking away*]: There was something between me and Yanek.

ANNENKOV: What do you mean? [*A pause.*]

STEPAN: I . . . envied him.

DORA: Go on, Stepan! What happened next?

STEPAN: Father Florentski held the crucifix out to him. . . . He refused to kiss it. He said: 'I've already told you that I've finished with life, and have come to terms with death.'

DORA: What was his voice like?

STEPAN: The same as always . . . but not so intense, not so impatient.

DORA: Did he look happy?

ANNENKOV: Are you mad?

DORA: Yes, he *did* look happy . . . I know he did! It would be too unfair if he did not find happiness in death when he had rejected it in life; he *was* happy . . . and he walked quite calmly to the scaffold, didn't he?

STEPAN: Yes. . . . Someone was singing to an accordion down on the river; just then a dog barked.

DORA: Then he . . .

STEPAN: He climbed the steps and was swallowed up by the darkness. You could just see the shroud which the hangman put over his head.

DORA: And then? [*A pause.*] What then? [*A pause.*]

STEPAN: Muffled sounds.

DORA: Muffled sounds! Oh, Yanek! And then? . . . [STEPAN *says nothing . . . violently.*] Tell me what happened next! . . . go on . . . [STEPAN *still says nothing.*] *You* tell me Alexis!

VOINOV: A . . . a horrible thud.

DORA: Aah! [*She flings herself against the wall . . .* STEPAN *turns away . . .* ANNENKOV *weeps, expressionless . . .* DORA *turns round and looks at them . . . leaning against the wall . . . in a changed, distraught voice.*] Don't cry . . . no, no, don't cry. Don't you realize . . . that today is the day of our justification! Something has been born today which is our testimony, the testimony of us revolutionaries. Yanek is no longer a murderer! A horrible thud! That's all it took . . . one thud and he was plunged back into the joys of childhood! Do you remember his laugh? He used to laugh sometimes . . . for no reason at all. . . . How young he was! He's laughing now . . . I know he is, his face pressed to the earth . . . [*She goes towards* ANNENKOV.] Boria? . . . you are my brother . . . you'll help me . . .

ANNENKOV: Yes, of course I will.

DORA: Then do this for me: let me throw the bomb . . . [ANNENKOV *looks at her.*] Yes . . . the next time, I want to throw the bomb . . . I want to be the first to throw it!

ANNENKOV: We don't let women throw the bombs.

DORA [*with a shriek*]: Am I a woman . . . now? [*They all look at her in silence.*]

VOINOV [*very quietly*]: Let her, Boria.

STEPAN: Yes, let her.

ANNENKOV: It's your turn, Stepan . . .

STEPAN [*looking at* DORA]: Let her. . . . She's . . . like me . . . now.

DORA: You will let me, won't you?

ANNENKOV: Yes, Dora.

DORA: I shall throw the bomb . . . and then one cold night . . . [*She cries uncontrollably.*] Oh, Yanek! . . . yes . . . one cold night . . . the same rope . . . everything will be easier . . . now. . . .

CURTAIN

THE POSSESSED

A Play in Three Parts

Based on the Novel by
FYODOR DOSTOIEVSKY

Translated from the French by
JUSTIN O'BRIEN

Foreword

THE POSSESSED is one of the four or five works that I rank above all others. In many ways I can claim that I grew up on it and took sustenance from it. For almost twenty years, in any event, I have visualized its characters on the stage. Besides having the stature of dramatic characters, they have the appropriate behaviour, the explosions, the swift and disconcerting gait. Moreover, Dostoievsky uses a theatre technique in his novels: he works through dialogues with few indications as to place and action. A man of the theatre – whether actor, producer, or author – always finds in him all the suggestions he needs.

And now THE POSSESSED has reached the stage after several years of labour and persistence. And yet I am well aware of all that separates the play from that amazing novel! I merely tried to follow the book's undercurrent and to proceed as it does from satiric comedy to drama and then to tragedy. Both the original and the dramatic adaptation start from a certain realism and end up in tragic stylization. As for the rest, I tried, amidst this vast, preposterous, panting world full of outbursts and scenes of violence, never to lose the thread of suffering and affection that makes Dostoievsky's universe so close to each of us. Dostoievsky's characters, as we know well by now, are neither odd nor absurd. They are like us; we have the same heart. And if THE POSSESSED is a prophetic book, this is not only because it prefigures our nihilism, but also because its protagonists are torn or dead souls unable to love and suffering from that inability, wanting to believe and yet unable to do so – like those who people our society and our spiritual world today. The subject of this work is just as much the murder of Shatov (inspired by a real event – the assassination of the student Ivanov by the nihilist Nechayev) as the spiritual adventure and death of Stavrogin, a contemporary hero. Hence we have dramatized not only one of the masterpieces of world literature but also a work of current application.

ALBERT CAMUS

N.B. The adaptation of THE POSSESSED reintegrates into the work Stavrogin's confession (which was not published because of censorship, though its place in the narrative is known to us) and utilizes the several hundred pages that make up the NOTEBOOKS of THE POSSESSED kept by the author while he was writing the novel.

Cast

GRIGORIEV, *the narrator*
STEPAN TROFIMOVICH VERKHOVENSKY
VARVARA PETROVNA STAVROGIN
LIPUTIN
SHIGALOV
IVAN SHATOV
VIRGINSKY
GAGANOV
ALEXEY YEGOROVICH
NICHOLAS STAVROGIN
PRASCOVYA DROZDOV
DASHA SHATOV
ALEXEY KIRILOV
LISA DROZDOV
MAURICE NICOLAEVICH
MARIA TIMOFEYEVNA LEBYATKIN
CAPTAIN LEBYATKIN
PETER STEPANOVICH VERKHOVENSKY
FEDKA
THE SEMINARIST
LYAMSHIN
BISHOP TIHON
GAGANOV'S SON
MARIA SHATOV

NOTE: *The necessities of stage production called for fairly numerous cuts in the text of the adaptation. This edition contains all the passages and scenes cut in the production. They have been set between parallel rules.*

Sets

1. At Varvara Stavrogin's. A luxurious period drawing-room.
2. Filipov's poor lodgings. Double set, representing a living-room and a small bedroom.
3. The street.

4. Lebyatkin's dwelling. A wretched living-room in the suburb.
5. The forest.
6. At Tihon's. A vast hall in the Convent of the Virgin.
7. The main drawing-room in the Stavrogin country house, at Skvoreshniki.

FIRST PART

When the theatre is altogether dark, a spotlight picks out the NARRATOR *standing in front of the curtain with hat in hand.*

ANTON GRIGORIEV, *the* NARRATOR [*courteous, calm and ironic*]:

Ladies and Gentlemen,

The strange events you are about to witness took place in our provincial city under the influence of my esteemed friend Professor Stepan Trofimovich Verkhovensky. The Professor had always played a thoroughly patriotic role among us. He was liberal and idealistic, loving the West, progress, justice, and generally everything lofty. But on those heights he unfortunately fell to imagining that the Tsar and his Ministers had a particular grudge against him, and he settled among us to play the part of the persecuted thinker in exile. It must be said that he did so with great dignity. Simply, three or four times a year he had attacks of patriotic melancholy that kept him in bed with a hot-water bottle on his belly.

He lived in the house of his friend Varvara Stavrogin, the widow of the General, who, after her husband's death, had entrusted to him the upbringing of her son, Nicholas Stavrogin. Oh, I forgot to tell you that Stepan Trofimovich was twice widowed and once a father. He had shipped his son abroad. Both his wives had died young, and, to tell the truth, they hadn't been very happy with him. But it is hardly possible to love one's wife and justice at the same time. Consequently, Stepan Trofimovich transferred all his affection to his pupil Nicholas Stavrogin, to whose moral education he applied himself most rigorously until Nicholas fled home and took to indulging in wild debauch. Hence, Stepan Trofimovich remained alone with Varvara Stavrogin, who felt an unlimited friendship for him – in other words, she often hated him. That is where my story begins.

SCENE ONE

The curtain rises on Varvara Stavrogin's drawing-room. The NARRATOR *goes over and sits down at the table to play cards with* STEPAN TROFIMOVICH.

STEPAN: Oh, I forgot to ask you to cut the cards. Forgive me, Anton, but I didn't sleep well at all last night. How I regretted having complained to you of Varvara!

GRIGORIEV: You merely said she was keeping you out of vanity and that she was jealous of your education.

STEPAN: That's what I mean. But it's not true! Your turn. You see, she's an angel of honour and sensitivity, and I'm just the reverse.

[VARVARA STAVROGIN *comes in, but stops at the door.*]

VARVARA: Cards again! [*They rise.*] Sit down and go on. I am busy. [*She goes over to look at some papers on a table at the left. They continue playing, but* STEPAN TROFIMOVICH *keeps glancing at* VARVARA STAVROGIN, *who finally speaks, avoiding his eyes.*] I thought you were to work on your book this morning.

STEPAN: I took a walk in the garden. I had taken Tocqueville under my arm –

VARVARA: And you read Paul de Kock instead. But you have been announcing your book for fifteen years now.

STEPAN: Yes, I have gathered the material, but I have to put it together. It doesn't matter anyway! I am forgotten. No one needs me.

VARVARA: You would be less forgotten if you played cards less often.

STEPAN: Yes, I play cards. And it's unworthy of me. But who is responsible? Who nipped my career in the bud? *Ah, que meure la Russie!* I'll trump that.

VARVARA: Nothing keeps you from working and from proving by your work that people were wrong to neglect you.

STEPAN: You are forgetting, *chère amie,* that I have published a great deal.

VARVARA: Indeed? Who remembers that now?

STEPAN: Who? Why, our friend here certainly remembers it.

GRIGORIEV: Of course I do. To begin with, your lectures on the nature of the Arabs, then the start of your study on the exceptional moral nobility of certain knights at a certain period, and, above all, your thesis on the importance that the small city of Hanau might have achieved between 1413 and 1428 if it had not been prevented from doing so by half-hidden causes, which you analysed brilliantly.

STEPAN: You have a memory like a steel trap, Anton. Thank you.

VARVARA: That is not the point. The point is that for fifteen years you have been announcing a book and you haven't written a single word of it.

STEPAN: Of course not, that would be too easy! I want to be sterile and solitary! That will teach them what they have lost. I want to be a living reproach!

VARVARA: You would be if you spent less time in bed.

STEPAN: What?

VARVARA: Yes, to be a living reproach one has to stand on one's feet.

STEPAN: Standing up or lying down, the important thing is to personify the idea. Besides, I am active, I am active, and always according to my principles. This very week I signed a protest.

VARVARA: Against what?

STEPAN: I don't know. It was . . . oh, I've forgotten. *Il fallait protester, voilà tout.* Oh, in my time everything was different. I used to work twelve hours a day . . .

VARVARA: Five or six would have been enough . . .

STEPAN: I used to spend hours in the library gathering mountains of notes. We had hope then! We used to talk until daybreak, building the future. Oh, how noble we were then, strong as steel, firm as the Rock of Gibraltar! Those were evenings truly worthy of Athens: music, Spanish melodies, love of humanity, the Sistine Madonna. . . . *O ma noble et fidèle amie,* have you any idea of all I gave up?

VARVARA: No. [*She rises.*] But I know that if you talked until dawn you couldn't work twelve hours a day. Besides, all this is mere talk! You know that at long last I am expecting my son, Nicholas, any moment. . . . I must have a word with you. [GRIGORIEV *gets up, comes over, and kisses her hand.*] Thank you, Anton, you are discreet. Stay in the garden and you can come back later.

[GRIGORIEV *leaves.*]

STEPAN: *Quel bonheur, ma noble amie, de revoir notre Nicolas!*

VARVARA: Yes, I am very happy. He is my whole life. But I am worried.

STEPAN: Worried?

VARVARA: Yes – don't act like a male nurse – I am worried. By the way, since when have you been wearing red neckties?

STEPAN: Why, just today I –

VARVARA: It doesn't suit your age, in my opinion. Where was I? Yes, I am worried. And you know very well why. All those rumours ... I can't believe them, and yet I can't forget them. Debauchery, violence, duels, he insults everybody, he frequents the dregs of society! Absurd, absurd! And yet, suppose it were true?

STEPAN: But it isn't possible. Just remember the dreamy, affectionate child he was. Just remember the touching melancholies he used to fall into. No one but an exceptional soul can feel such melancholy ... as I am well aware.

VARVARA: You are forgetting that he is no longer a child.

||STEPAN: But his health is poor. Just remember; he used to weep for nights on end. Can you imagine him forcing men to fight?

VARVARA: He was in no way weak! What has made you imagine that? He was simply high-strung, that's all. But you got it into your head to wake him up in the middle of the night, when he was twelve years old, to tell him your troubles. That's the kind of tutor you were.

STEPAN: *Le cher ange* loved me. He used to ask me to confide in him and would weep in my arms.

VARVARA: The angel has changed. I am told that I wouldn't recognize him now, that his physical strength is exceptional. ||

STEPAN: But what does he tell you in his letters?

VARVARA: His letters are few and far between but always respectful.

STEPAN: You see?

VARVARA: I see nothing. You should get out of the habit of talking without saying anything. And, besides, the facts speak for themselves. Did he or didn't he have his commission taken away from him because he had seriously wounded another officer in a duel?

STEPAN: That's not a crime. He was motivated by the warmth of his noble blood. That's all very chivalrous.

VARVARA: Yes. But it is less chivalrous to live in the vilest sections of St Petersburg and to enjoy the company of cut-throats and drunkards.

STEPAN [*laughing*]: Oh, that's simply Prince Harry's youth all over again!

VARVARA: What do you mean by that?

STEPAN: Why, Shakespeare, *ma noble amie,* immortal Shakespeare, the genius of geniuses, great Will, in short, who shows us Prince Harry indulging in debauch with his friend Falstaff.

VARVARA: I shall re-read the play. By the way, are you taking any exercise? You are well aware that you should walk six versts a day. Good. In any case, I asked Nicholas to come home. I want you to sound him out. I plan to keep him here and to arrange his marriage.

STEPAN: His marriage! Oh, how romantic that is! Have you anyone in mind?

VARVARA: Yes, I am thinking of Lisa, the daughter of my friend Prascovya Drozdov. They are in Switzerland with my ward, Dasha.... But what does it matter to you?

STEPAN: I love Nicholas as much as my own son.

VARVARA: That isn't much. Altogether, you have seen your son only twice, including the day of his birth.

STEPAN: His aunts brought him up and I sent him regularly the income from the little estate his mother left him, and all the time I suffered bitterly from his absence. Moreover, he's a complete dud, poor in spirit and poor in heart. You should see the letters he writes me! You would think he was speaking to a servant. I asked him with all my paternal love if he didn't want to come and see me. Do you know what he replied? 'If I come home, it will be to check my accounts, and to settle accounts too.'

VARVARA: Why don't you learn once and for all to make people respect you? Well, I shall leave you. It is time for your little gathering. Your friends, your little spree, cards, atheism, and, above all, the stench, the stench of tobacco and of men ... I am leaving. Don't drink too much, you know it upsets you.... Good-bye! [*She looks at him; then shrugging her shoulders:*] A red necktie! [*She leaves.*]

STEPAN [*follows her with his eyes, starts to stammer, then looks towards the desk*]: *O femme cruelle, implacable!* And I can't talk to her! I shall write her a letter! [*He goes towards the table.*]

VARVARA [*thrusting her head in the door*]: And, by the way, stop writing me letters. We live in the same house; it is ridiculous to exchange letters. Your friends are here.

[*She leaves.* GRIGORIEV, LIPUTIN, *and* SHIGALOV *come in.*]

STEPAN: Good day, my dear Liputin, good day. Forgive my emotion.... I am hated.... Yes, I am literally hated. But I don't care! Your wife is not with you?

LIPUTIN: No. Wives must stay at home and fear God.

STEPAN: But aren't you an atheist?

LIPUTIN: Yes. Shhhh! Don't say it so loud. That's just it. A husband who is an atheist must teach his wife the fear of God. That liberates him even more. Look at our friend Virginsky. I met him just now. He had to go out and do his marketing himself because his wife was with Captain Lebyatkin.

STEPAN: Yes, yes, I know what people say, but it's not true. His wife is a noble creature. Besides, they all are.

LIPUTIN: What, not true? I was told it by Virginsky himself. He converted his wife to our ideas. He convinced her that man is a free creature, or ought to be such. So she freed herself and, later on, simply told Virginsky that she was dismissing him as her husband and taking Captain Lebyatkin in his place. And do you know what Virginsky said to his wife when she announced this news? He said: 'My dear, up to now I merely loved you; from now on, I esteem you.'

STEPAN: He's a true Roman.

GRIGORIEV: I was told, on the contrary, that when his wife dismissed him, he burst into sobs.

STEPAN: Yes, yes. He's an affectionate soul. [SHATOV *comes in.*] But here's our friend Shatov. Any news of your sister?

SHATOV: Dasha is about to come home. Since you ask me, I shall tell you that she is bored in Switzerland with Prascovya Drozdov and Lisa. I am telling you, although in my opinion it is no concern of yours.

STEPAN: Of course not. But she is coming home, and that is the main thing. Oh, my dear friends, it's impossible to live far from Russia –

LIPUTIN: But it's impossible to live in Russia, too. We need something else, and there is nothing.

STEPAN: What do you suggest?

LIPUTIN: Everything must be made over.

SHIGALOV: Yes, but you don't draw the conclusions. [SHATOV *goes over and sits down gloomily and places his cap beside him.* VIRGINSKY *and then* GAGANOV *come in.*]

STEPAN: Good day, my dear Virginsky. How is your wife?

... [VIRGINSKY *turns away.*] Good, we're fond of you, you know, very fond of you!

GAGANOV: I was just going by and I came in to see Varvara Stavrogin. But perhaps I am in your way?

STEPAN: No, no! *Au banquet de l'amitié* there is always room. We were just beginning to discuss things. I know you are not afraid of a few paradoxes.

GAGANOV: Aside from the Tsar, Russia, and the family, everything is open to discussion. [*To* SHATOV] Don't you agree?

SHATOV: Everything is open to discussion. But certainly not with you.

STEPAN [*laughing*]: We must drink to the conversion of our good friend Gaganov. [*He rings a bell.*] That is, if Shatov, irascible Shatov, allows us to. For our good Shatov is irascible; he boils over at nothing at all. And if you want to discuss with him, you have to tie him down first. You see, he's already leaving. He has taken offence. Come, come now, my good friend, you know how fond we are of you.

SHATOV: Then don't insult me.

STEPAN: But who is insulting you? If I did so, I beg your pardon. I am well aware that we talk too much. We talk when we ought to act. Act, act ... or, in any case, work. For twenty years now I have been sounding the alarm and urging people to work. Russia can't arise without ideas. And we can't have ideas without working. Let's get down to work, then, and eventually we'll have an original idea ...

[ALEXEY YEGOROVICH, *the butler, brings in drinks and leaves.*]

LIPUTIN: Meanwhile, we should suppress the army and the navy.

GAGANOV: Both at once?

LIPUTIN: Yes, in order to have universal peace!

GAGANOV: But if others don't suppress theirs, wouldn't they be tempted to invade us? How can we know?

LIPUTIN: By suppressing ours. In that way we shall know.

STEPAN [*quivering with excitement*]: *Ah! C'est un paradoxe!* But there is truth in it...

VIRGINSKY: Liputin goes too far because he despairs of ever seeing our ideas dominate. *I* think we should begin at the beginning and get rid of priests and the family at the same time.

GAGANOV: Gentlemen, I can take any joke whatever... but to suppress at one and the same time the army, the navy, the family, the priests – no, no, no.

STEPAN: There's no harm in talking about it. One can talk of anything.

GAGANOV: But to suppress everything like that all at once – no. Ah, no. No...

LIPUTIN: Come, now. Don't you think Russia needs reform?

GAGANOV: Yes, probably. Everything isn't perfect in our country.

LIPUTIN: Then it must be dismembered.

STEPAN *and* GAGANOV: What?

LIPUTIN: Yes, of course. To reform Russia, it has to be made into a federation. But before it can be federated, it has to be dismembered. It's mathematically simple.

STEPAN: It deserves reflection.

GAGANOV: I.... Oh, no, I won't let anyone lead me around by the nose...

VIRGINSKY: Reflection calls for time, and abject poverty can't wait.

LIPUTIN: We must think of the most urgent first. The most urgent need is for everyone to be able to eat. Books, art galleries, theatres are for later on, later on. . . . A pair of shoes is worth more than Shakespeare.

STEPAN: Oh, I can't admit this. No, no, my good friend, immortal genius shines over all mankind. Let everyone go barefoot and long live Shakespeare . . .

SHIGALOV: You don't any of you draw the conclusions.

[*He leaves.*]

LIPUTIN: Allow me –

STEPAN: No, no, I cannot accept that. *Nous qui aimons le peuple* –

SHATOV: You don't love the masses.

VIRGINSKY: What? I –

SHATOV [*rising in anger*]: You don't love either Russia or the masses. You have lost contact with the masses. You talk about them as if they were a distant tribe with exotic customs that move you to pity. You have lost track of them, and without the masses, there is no god. This is why all of you and all of us, yes, all of us, are so wretchedly cold and indifferent. We are merely out of step, nothing else. You yourself, Stepan Trofimovich, I make no exception for you, let it be known, although you taught us all. In fact, I am speaking especially to you.

[*He seizes his cap and rushes towards the door. But* STEPAN TROFIMOVICH *calls out to stop him.*]

STEPAN: All right, Shatov, since you insist, I am angry with you. Now let us make it up. [*He holds out his hand, and* SHATOV *reluctantly shakes it.*] Let's drink to universal reconciliation!

GAGANOV: Let's drink. But I won't let anyone lead me around by the nose.

[*Toast.* VARVARA STAVROGIN *enters.*]

VARVARA: Please don't get up. Drink to the health of my son, Nicholas, who has just arrived. He has gone up to change, and I have asked him to come and say hello to your friends.

STEPAN: How did he seem to you, *ma noble amie?*

VARVARA: His appearance and good health delighted me. [*She looks at them.*] Yes, why not say so? There have been so many rumours recently that I am glad to have a chance to show what my son is.

GAGANOV: We are delighted to see him, my dear!

VARVARA [*looking at* SHATOV]: And you, Shatov, are you happy to see your friend again? [SHATOV *gets up and, as he does so, awkwardly knocks over a small intarsia table.*] Pick up that table, please. It will be chipped, but there's no use crying over that. [*To the others.*] What were you talking about?

STEPAN: Of hope, *ma noble amie,* and of the luminous future already visible at the end of our dark way.... Oh, we shall be consoled for such sufferings and persecutions. Exile will come to an end, for dawn is already in sight...

[NICHOLAS STAVROGIN *appears upstage and stands still on the threshold.*]

STEPAN: *Ah, mon cher enfant!*

[VARVARA *makes a move towards* STAVROGIN, *but his unemotional manner stops her. She looks at him with anguish. A few seconds of general embarrassment.*]

GAGANOV: How are you, my dear Nicholas?

STAVROGIN: I am well, thank you.

[*A merry scene of greeting ensues.* STAVROGIN *steps towards his mother and kisses her hand.* STEPAN TROFIMOVICH *goes up to him and embraces him,* STAVROGIN *smiles at* STEPAN *and resumes his unemotional manner while the others, except* SHATOV, *greet him. But his prolonged silence dampens the enthusiasm.*]

VARVARA [*looking at* NICHOLAS]: Dear, dear child, you are sad, you are bored. That is right.

STEPAN [*bringing him a glass*]: My good Nicholas!

VARVARA: Go on, I beg you. We were talking of the dawn. I believe.

[STAVROGIN *lifts his glass as a toast in the direction of* SHATOV, *who leaves the room without saying a word.* STAVROGIN *sniffs the contents of his glass and sets it down on the table without drinking it.*]

LIPUTIN [*after a moment of general embarrassment*]: Good. Did you know that the new governor had already arrived?

[*In his corner on the left,* VIRGINSKY *says something to* GAGANOV, *who answers:*]

GAGANOV: I won't let anyone lead me around by the nose.

LIPUTIN: It seems that he wants to upset everything. But it would surprise me if he did.

STEPAN: It won't last. Just a touch of administrative intoxication!

[STAVROGIN *has gone over to the spot vacated by* SHATOV. *Standing very upright with a far-away, gloomy look on his face, he is watching* GAGANOV.]

VARVARA: What do you mean now?

STEPAN: Why, you know the symptoms, don't you? For instance, just entrust any old nitwit with selling tickets behind the window of the most insignificant station and immediately, when you go to get a ticket, that nitwit will look at you as if he were Jupiter, just to show his power. The nitwit is drunk, you see. He is suffering from administrative intoxication.

VARVARA: Come to the point, I beg you.

STEPAN: I simply meant. . . . However that may be, I know the new governor somewhat. A very handsome man, isn't he – about forty years old?

VARVARA: Where did you get the idea that he is a handsome man? He has pop eyes.

STEPAN: That's true, but. . . .Well, in any case, I accept the opinion of the ladies.

GAGANOV: We can't criticize the new governor before seeing him at work, can we?

LIPUTIN: And why shouldn't we criticize him? He's the governor; isn't that enough?

GAGANOV: Allow me –

VIRGINSKY: It's through reasoning like Gaganov's that Russia is sinking into ignorance. If a horse were named governor, Gaganov would wait to see him at work.

GAGANOV: Oh! But, allow me, you are insulting me, and I won't permit it. I said . . . or, rather . . . I repeat: I won't let anyone lead me around by the nose . . . [STAVROGIN *crosses the stage amid the silence that sets in with his first step, advances like a sleepwalker towards* GAGANOV, *slowly raises his arm, seizes* GAGANOV'*s nose, and, gently pulling it, makes* GAGANOV *step towards the centre of the stage. With anguish in her voice,* VARVARA STAVROGIN *shouts:* 'Nicholas!' NICHOLAS *lets go of* GAGANOV, *steps backwards a few steps, and looks at him, smiling absent-mindedly. After a second of stupor, general tumult. The others surround* GAGANOV *and lead him to a chair, into which he sinks.* NICHOLAS STAVROGIN *turns on his heels and leaves the room.* VARVARA STAVROGIN, *hardly knowing what she is doing, takes up a glass and carries it over to* GAGANOV.] He. . . . How could he . . .? Help, help!

VARVARA [*to* STEPAN TROFIMOVICH]: Oh, my God, he's mad, he's mad!

STEPAN [*hardly knowing what he is doing either*]: No, *très chère,* mere thoughtlessness, youth . . .

VARVARA [*to* GAGANOV]: Forgive Nicholas, my friend, I beg of you.

[STAVROGIN *enters. After a brief hesitation he walks firmly towards* GAGANOV, *who gets up, frightened. Then rapidly and with a frown:*]

STAVROGIN: Of course you will forgive me! A sudden whim. . . . A stupid distraction . . .

STEPAN [*stepping up to the other side of* STAVROGIN, *who is looking vacantly ahead of him*]: That's not an acceptable apology, Nicholas. [*With anguish*] *Je vous en prie, mon enfant.* You have a noble heart, you are well brought up and cultured, and suddenly you seem to us enigmatic – a dangerous person. At least have pity on your mother.

STAVROGIN [*looking at his mother, then at* GAGANOV]: All right. I shall apologize. But I shall do so secretly to Mr Gaganov, who will understand me.

[GAGANOV *steps forward hesitantly.* STAVROGIN *leans over and seizes* GAGANOV'*s ear in his teeth.*]

GAGANOV [*in pain*]: Nicholas! Nicholas!

[*The others, who haven't yet understood the situation, look at him.*]

GAGANOV [*in terror*]: Nicholas, you are biting my ear! [*Screaming.*] He's biting my ear! [STAVROGIN *lets go of him and stands staring at him with a dull look on his face.* GAGANOV *rushes out, screaming with fright.*] Watch out! Watch out!

VARVARA [*going to her son*]: Nicholas, for the love of God!

[NICHOLAS *looks at her, laughs weakly, then collapses on the floor in a sort of fit.*]

BLACKOUT

THE NARRATOR: Gaganov stayed in bed several weeks. Nicholas Stavrogin likewise. But he eventually got up, made his apologies most honourably, and set out for a rather long trip. The only place where he stayed for a time was Geneva – not because of the hectic charm of that city, but because there he found the Drozdov ladies.

SCENE TWO

Varvara Stavrogin's drawing-room. VARVARA STAVROGIN *and* PRASCOVYA DROZDOV *are on the stage.*

PRASCOVYA: Oh, my dear, I can say that I am pleased to return Dasha Shatov to you. I have no criticism to make, for my part, but it seems to me that if she hadn't been there, there would not have been that little misunderstanding between your Nicholas and my Lisa. I assure you that I know nothing, for Lisa is much too proud, too obstinate, to have spoken to me. But the fact is that they are at odds with each other, that Lisa was humiliated, God alone knows why, and that perhaps your Dasha would have something to say about it, although . . .

VARVARA: I don't like insinuations, Prascovya. Tell all you have to tell. Are you trying to imply that Dasha had an intrigue with Nicholas?

PRASCOVYA: An intrigue, dear – what a word! Besides, I don't want to imply . . . I love you too much. . . . How can you imagine? . . . [*She dries a tear.*]

VARVARA: Don't weep. I'm not hurt. Just tell me what took place.

PRASCOVYA: Why, nothing at all. He is in love with Lisa, that's certain. I couldn't be mistaken on that point. Feminine intuition! . . . But you know Lisa's character. I suppose one might say obstinate and scornful – yes, that's it! And Nicholas is proud. What pride – oh, he is indeed your son! Well, he couldn't put up with her little jokes. And, in return, he bantered.

VARVARA: Bantered?

PRASCOVYA: Yes, that's the word. In any case, Lisa constantly tried to start a quarrel with Nicholas. Sometimes when she was aware that he was talking with Dasha, you couldn't hold her back. Really, my dear, it was unbearable. The doctors forbade me to get excited, and, furthermore, I was so bored on the shores of that lake, and I had a toothache. Since then I have learned that the Lake of Geneva predisposes people to toothaches, and that that's one of its peculiarities. Finally Nicholas left. In my opinion, they will make it up.

VARVARA: Such a slight misunderstanding doesn't mean a thing. Besides, I know my Dasha too well. It's utterly absurd. Moreover, I shall get at the facts of the matter.

[*She rings.*]

PRASCOVYA: No, I assure you...

[ALEXEY YEGOROVICH *enters.*]

VARVARA: Tell Dasha that I am waiting for her.

[ALEXEY YEGOROVICH *leaves.*]

PRASCOVYA: I was wrong, dear, to speak to you of Dasha. There was nothing but the most ordinary conversations between her and Nicholas, and there was no whispering. At least in my presence. But I felt Lisa's irritation. And then that lake – you have no idea! It does calm you, to be sure, but only because it bores you. Yet, if you know what I mean, simply by boring you it irritates you... [DASHA *enters.*] My Dashenka, my little one! How I hate giving you up. We shall miss our good evening conversations in Geneva. Oh! Geneva! *Au revoir, chère!* [*To* DASHA] *Au revoir, ma mignonne, ma chérie, ma colombe.* [*She leaves.*]

VARVARA: Sit down there. [DASHA *sits down.*] Embroider. [DASHA *picks up an embroidery frame from the table.*] Tell me about your trip.

DASHA [*in a steady, dull voice, somewhat tired*]: Oh! I had a good time, and I learned a great deal. Europe is very instructive – yes, instructive. We are so far behind them. They –

VARVARA: Forget Europe. You have nothing particular to tell me?

DASHA [*looks at her*]: No, nothing.

VARVARA: Nothing on your mind, or on your conscience, or in your heart?

DASHA [*with a sort of colourless conviction*]: Nothing.

VARVARA: I was sure of it. I never had the slightest doubt about you. I have treated you as my daughter, and I am aiding your brother. You wouldn't do anything that might hurt me, would you?

DASHA: No, nothing, God bless you.

VARVARA: Listen. I have been thinking about you. Drop your embroidery and come over near me. [DASHA *moves closer to her.*] Do you want to get married? [DASHA *looks at her.*] Wait a moment, don't answer. I am thinking of someone older than you. But you are a reasonable girl. Besides, he is still very presentable. I am thinking of Stepan Trofimovich who was your professor and whom you have always esteemed. Well? [DASHA *keeps on looking at her fixedly.*] I know, he is frivolous. He whimpers and he thinks about himself too much. But he has decided qualities that you will appreciate, particularly because I ask it of you. He deserves to be loved because he is defenceless. Do you understand that? [DASHA *nods affirmatively. Bursting out*] I was sure of it; I was sure of you. As for him, he will love you because he is under an obligation! He must adore you! Listen, Dasha. He will obey you. Unless you are an idiot, you can force him to. But never push him to extremes – that is the first rule of conjugal life. Oh, Dasha, there is no greater happiness than sacrificing oneself. Besides, you will be doing me a great favour, and that is the important thing. But I am not forcing you in any way. It is up to you to decide. Speak.

DASHA [*slowly*]: If it is absolutely necessary, I shall do it.

VARVARA: Absolutely? What are you alluding to, my child? [DASHA *lowers her head in silence.*] What you have just said is a stupidity. I am going to marry you off, to be sure, but not out of necessity, you understand. The idea just came to me, that's all. There's nothing to hide, is there?

DASHA: No. I shall do as you wish.

VARVARA: Hence you consent. So let's get to the details. Directly after the ceremony, I shall give you fifteen thousand roubles. Out of those fifteen thousand, you will give eight thousand to Stepan Trofimovich. Allow him to receive his friends once a week. If they should come more often, put them out. Moreover, I shall be there to keep an eye on things.

DASHA: Has Stepan Trofimovich said anything to you about this?

VARVARA: No, he hasn't said anything. But he will. [*She rises suddenly and throws her black shawl over her shoulders.* DASHA *continues to stare at her.*] You are an ungrateful girl! What are you thinking of? Do you think I am going to compromise you? Why, he will come on his knees to beg you to marry him! He will be bursting with happiness, that's how it will be!

[STEPAN TROFIMOVICH *enters.* DASHA *rises.*]

STEPAN: Oh! Dashenka, my pretty girl, what a delight to

find you among us again. [*He kisses her.*] Here you are at last!

VARVARA: Leave her alone. You have all of life ahead of you to caress her. And I have something to say to you.
[DASHA *leaves.*]

STEPAN: *Soit, mon amie, soit.* But you know how much I love my little pupil.

VARVARA: I know. But don't keep calling her 'my little pupil'. She is grown-up! It's irritating! Hum, you have been smoking.

STEPAN: *C'est-à-dire* . . .

VARVARA: Sit down. That's not the question. The question is that you must get married.

STEPAN [*stupefied*]: Get married? A third time, and at the age of fifty-three!

VARVARA: Well, what difference does that make? At fifty-three we are at the peak of life. I know what I am saying, for I am almost there. Besides, you are a handsome man.

STEPAN: You have always been indulgent towards me, *mon amie. Mais je dois vous dire . . . je ne m'attendais pas.* . . . Yes, at the age of fifty we are not yet old. That is obvious.
[*He looks at her.*]

VARVARA: I shall help you. She will not be without a dowry. Oh! I forgot: you are marrying Dasha.

STEPAN [*giving a start*]: Dasha. . . . But I thought . . . Dasha! But she's only a child!

VARVARA: A twenty-year-old child, *grâce à Dieu!* Don't roll your eyes that way, please; you're not in the circus. You are intelligent, but you don't understand anything. You need someone to take care of you constantly. What will you do if I die? Dasha will be an excellent housekeeper for you. Moreover, I shall be there; I'm not going to die right away. Besides, she is an angel of kindness. [*Bursting out in anger*] You understand, I am telling you that she is an angel of kindness!

STEPAN: I know, but such a difference in age ... I was thinking.... If necessary, you see, someone of my own age...

VARVARA: Well, you will educate her, you will develop her heart. You will give her an honourable name. Perhaps you will be her saviour – yes, her saviour...

STEPAN: But what about her? ... Have you talked to her?

VARVARA: Don't worry about her. Of course, it is up to you to urge her, to beg her to do you that honour, you understand. But don't worry, for *I* shall be there. Besides, you love her. [STEPAN TROFIMOVICH *rises and staggers.*] What's the matter with you?

STEPAN: I ... I accept, of course, of course, because you wish it, but I should never have thought that you would agree...

VARVARA: What do you mean?

STEPAN: Without an overriding reason, without an urgent reason ... I should never have thought that you could accept seeing me married to ... to another woman.

VARVARA [*rises suddenly*]: Another woman! [*She looks at him with flashing eyes, then heads towards the door. Before reaching it, she turns to him.*] I shall never forgive you, never, you understand, for having imagined for one second that between you and me ... [*She is on the point of leaving, but* GRIGORIEV *enters.*] I.... Good day, Grigoriev. [*To* STEPAN TROFIMOVICH] So you have accepted. I shall arrange the details myself. Moreover, I am on my way to Prascovya's to tell her about the plan. And take care of yourself. Don't let yourself get any older! [*She leaves.*]

GRIGORIEV: Our friend seems thoroughly upset.

STEPAN: In other words.... Oh, I shall eventually lose all patience and cease wanting...

GRIGORIEV: Wanting what?

STEPAN: I agreed because I am bored with life and nothing matters to me. But if she exasperates me, things might begin to matter to me. I shall be aware of the insult and I shall refuse.

GRIGORIEV: You will refuse?

STEPAN: To get married. Oh, I shouldn't have talked about it! But you are my friend; it is as if I were talking to myself. Yes, I am asked to marry Dasha, and I accepted in principle, I accepted. At my age! Oh, my dear friend, for any soul that is the least bit proud, the least bit free, marriage is death itself. Marriage will corrupt me and sap my energy; I shall no longer be able to serve the cause of humanity. Children will come, and God alone will know whether they are mine. No, after all, they won't be mine; the wise man can face the truth. And I have accepted! Because I am bored. No, it's not because I am bored that I accepted. But there's that debt...

GRIGORIEV: You are doing yourself an injustice. A man doesn't have to need money to marry a pretty young girl.

STEPAN: Alas, I need money more than I need a pretty girl....You know that I didn't manage very well that property my son inherited from his mother. He is going to demand the eight thousand roubles I owe him. He is accused of being a revolutionary, a socialist, of aiming to destroy God and property, and so forth. I don't know about God, but as for property, he clings to his own, I assure you.... Besides, it's a debt of honour for me. I must sacrifice myself.

GRIGORIEV: But all this does you honour. Why are you complaining?

STEPAN: There's something else in it. I suspect.... Well.... Oh, I am not as stupid as I seem in her presence! Why this marriage in haste? Dasha was in Switzerland. She saw Nicholas. And now...

GRIGORIEV: I don't understand.

STEPAN: Yes, there's a mystery about it. Why such a mystery? I don't want to cover up the sins of others. Yes, the sins of others! O God who art so great and so good who will console me!

[LISA *and* MAURICE NICOLAEVICH *enter.*]

LISA: Here he is at last, Maurice, this is he, this is the man. [*To* STEPAN TROFIMOVICH] You recognize me, don't you?

STEPAN: *Dieu! Dieu! Chère Lisa!* At last a minute of happiness!

LISA: Yes. It's been twelve years since we have seen each other. And you are happy, aren't you, to see me again? You haven't forgotten your little pupil?

[STEPAN TROFIMOVICH *rushes towards her, seizes her hand, and stares at her, unable to speak.*]

LISA: Here are some flowers for you. I wanted to bring you a cake, but Maurice Nicolaevich advised flowers. He has such a sense of propriety. This is Maurice: I should like you to become good friends. I like him very much. Yes, he is the man I like most in the world. Maurice, I want you to meet my dear old professor.

MAURICE: I feel most honoured.

LISA [*to* STEPAN]: What a delight to see you again! And yet I am sad. Why do I always feel sad at such moments? You are such a learned man – can't you tell me? I always imagined that I should be madly happy when I saw you again and that I should remember everything, and here I am not at all happy – and, yet, I love you.

STEPAN [*with the flowers in his hand*]: It doesn't matter. Here I am too, loving you dearly, and you see I'm on the point of weeping.

LISA: Why, you have my portrait on the wall! [*She goes and takes down a miniature.*] Can this be I? Was I really so pretty? But I won't look at it! One life ends, another begins, then it yields to still another, and so on *ad infinitum.* [*Looking at* GRIGORIEV] You see how all this calls up the past!

STEPAN: Forgive me, I was forgetting to introduce Grigoriev, an excellent old friend.

LISA [*with a touch of coquetry*]: Oh, yes, you are the confidant! I like you very much.

GRIGORIEV: I don't deserve such an honour.

LISA: Come, now, don't be ashamed of being a good man. [*She turns her back on him and he looks at her with admiration.*] Dasha came back with us. But you know that already, of course. She's a dear, I should like her to be happy. By the way, she told me a lot about her brother. What is Shatov like?

STEPAN: Well, he's a dreamer! He was a socialist, then he abjured his ideas, and now he lives according to God and Russia.

LISA: Yes, someone told me that he was a bit odd. I want to know him. I should like to give him some work to do.

STEPAN: Indeed, that would be a godsend for him.

LISA: A godsend – why? I want to know him; I am interested. ... I mean, I really need someone to help me.

GRIGORIEV: I know Shatov rather well, and, if I can help you, I'll go and see him at once.

LISA: Yes, yes. I may even go myself. Although I don't want

to disturb him, nor anyone else in that house. But we will have to be back home in a quarter of an hour. Are you ready, Maurice?

MAURICE: I am at your beck and call.

LISA: Splendid. You are good. [*To* STEPAN TROFIMOVICH *as she goes towards the door*] I imagine you are like me: I detest men who are not good, even if they are very handsome and very intelligent. The important thing is a good heart. By the way, let me congratulate you on your marriage.

STEPAN: What, you know?

LISA: Of course. Varvara has just told us. What good news! And I am sure that Dasha was not expecting it. Come, Maurice...

BLACKOUT

THE NARRATOR: So I went to see Shatov because Lisa wanted me to and it already seemed to me that I could refuse her nothing, although I did not for a moment believe the explanations she gave for her sudden whim. This took me, and takes you likewise, to a less elegant section of town where the landlady Filipov let out rooms and a common living-room to odd individuals such as Lebyatkin and his sister Maria, Shatov, and, above all, the engineer Kirilov.

SCENE THREE

The scene shows a living-room and a small bedroom, Shatov's, on the right. The living-room has a door on the left opening into Kirilov's room and two doors upstage, one for the outer entrance and the other opening on to the stairs leading to the upper storey. In the centre of the living-room KIRILOV, *facing the audience, is doing his exercises with a most serious look on his face.*

KIRILOV: One, two, three, four . . . One, two, three, four . . . [*He takes a deep breath.*] One, two, three, four . . .

[GRIGORIEV *enters.*]

GRIGORIEV: Am I disturbing you? I was looking for Ivan Shatov.

KIRILOV: He is out. You are not disturbing me, but I still have one exercise to do. Allow me. [*He goes through his exercise, muttering numbers as he does so.*] There, Shatov will be back soon. May I give you some tea? I like drinking tea at night. Especially after my exercises. I walk a great deal, up and down, and I drink tea until dawn.

GRIGORIEV: Do you go to bed at dawn?

KIRILOV: Always. I have for a long time. At night I reflect.

GRIGORIEV: All night long?

KIRILOV [*calmly*]: Yes, it is essential. You see, I am concerned with the reasons why men don't dare kill themselves.

GRIGORIEV: Don't dare? In your opinion, there are not enough suicides?

KIRILOV [*absent-minded*]: Normally, there ought to be many more.

GRIGORIEV [*ironically*]: And what, in your opinion, keeps people from killing themselves?

KIRILOV: The pain. Those who kill themselves through madness or despair don't think of the pain. But those who kill themselves through reason obviously think of it.

GRIGORIEV: What, are there people who kill themselves through reason?

KIRILOV: Many. Were it not for the pain and the prejudice, there would be many more, a very large number, probably all men.

GRIGORIEV: What?

KIRILOV: But the idea that they will suffer keeps them from killing themselves. Even when one knows there is no pain, the idea remains. Just imagine a stone as big as a house falling on you. You wouldn't have time to feel anything, to suffer at all. Well, even so, men are afraid and hesitate. It is interesting.

GRIGORIEV: There must be another reason.

KIRILOV: Yes. . . . The other world.

GRIGORIEV: You mean punishment.

KIRILOV: No, the other world. People think there is a reason for going on living.

GRIGORIEV: And there isn't any?

KIRILOV: No, there is none, and that's why we are free. It is a matter of indifference whether we live or die.

GRIGORIEV: How can you say that so calmly?

KIRILOV: I don't like getting into disputes, and I never laugh.

GRIGORIEV: Man is afraid of death because he likes life, because life is good, that's all.

KIRILOV [*suddenly bursting out*]: But that's cowardice, just cowardice! Life isn't good. And the other world does not exist! God is simply a ghost conjured up by fear of death and suffering. In order to be free, it is essential to overcome pain and terror, it is essential to kill oneself. Then there will no longer be any God, and man will at last be free. Then history will be divided into two parts: from the ape to the destruction of God, and from the destruction of God . . .

GRIGORIEV: To the ape.

KIRILOV: To the divinity of man. [*Suddenly calm*] The man who dares to kill himself is God. No one had ever thought of that. But *I* have.

GRIGORIEV: There have been millions of suicides.

KIRILOV: Never for that reason. Always from fear. Never to kill fear. The man who kills himself to kill fear will at that very moment become God.

GRIGORIEV: I am afraid he won't have time.

KIRILOV [*rising and slowly with scorn in his voice*]: I am sorry that you seem to be laughing.

GRIGORIEV: Forgive me; I wasn't laughing. But it is all so strange.

KIRILOV: Why strange? The strange thing is that people can live without thinking of that. *I* can't think of anything else. All my life I have thought of nothing else. [*He gestures to* GRIGORIEV, *who leans forward.*] All my life I have been tormented by God.

GRIGORIEV: Why do you speak to me like this? You don't know me.

KIRILOV: You look like my brother, who died seven years ago.

GRIGORIEV: Did he exert a great influence over you?

KIRILOV: No. He never said anything. But you look very much like him, extraordinarily like him. [SHATOV *comes in.* KIRILOV *rises.*] I beg to inform you that Mr Grigoriev has been waiting for you for some time. [*He leaves.*]

SHATOV: What's the matter with him?

GRIGORIEV: I don't know. If I understood what he was saying, he wants all of us to commit suicide to prove to God that He doesn't exist.

SHATOV: Yes, he's a nihilist. He caught the bug in America.

GRIGORIEV: In America?

SHATOV: That's where I met him. We starved together and slept together on the bare ground. ||That was the time when I felt the same as all those thwarted people. We wanted to go there to experience directly how it feels to be placed in the worst social conditions.

GRIGORIEV: Good Lord! Why go so far? All you had to do was sign up for the harvest twenty kilometres from here.

SHATOV: I know. But that's how mad we were. Kirilov hasn't changed, although there is in him a deep passion and a resistance that I respect. In America he starved without a word of complaint. || Fortunately, a generous friend sent us money to get back home. [*He looks fixedly at the* NARRATOR.] You don't ask who that man was?

GRIGORIEV: Who?

SHATOV: Nicholas Stavrogin. [*Silence.*] And you probably think you know why he did it?

GRIGORIEV: I pay no attention to gossip.

SHATOV: Well, even if he did have an affair with my wife? [*He stares at him.*] I haven't yet paid him back. But I shall do so. I don't want to have anything to do with such people. [*Pause.*] You see, Grigoriev, all those people, Liputin, Shigalov, and so many others, like Stepan Trofimovich's son and even Stavrogin – you know what motivates them? Hatred. [*The* NARRATOR *makes a gesture of protest.*] Yes. They hate their country. They would be the first to suffer dreadfully if their country could be suddenly reformed, if it became exceptionally prosperous and happy. They wouldn't have anyone to spit on any more. Whereas now they can spit on their country and wish her all kinds of misfortune.

GRIGORIEV: And you, Shatov?

SHATOV: I love Russia now, although I am not worthy of her. That is why I am saddened by her misfortune and my own unworthiness. And they, my former friends, accuse me of having betrayed them. [*He turns away.*]

Meanwhile, I ought to earn some money to repay Stavrogin. I absolutely must.

GRIGORIEV: It so happens –

[*There is a knock at the door.* SHATOV *goes to open it.* LISA *enters with a bundle of newspapers under her arm.*]

LISA [*to* GRIGORIEV]: Oh, you are already here! [*She goes towards him.*] So I was right when I thought yesterday at Stepan Trofimovich's that you would help me. Have you had a chance to talk to this Mr Shatov? [*Meanwhile, she has been looking eagerly around her.*]

GRIGORIEV: Here he is. But I haven't had time.... Shatov, Elizabeth Drozdov, whom you know by name, has asked me to talk to you about something.

LISA: I am happy to know you. I have heard about you. Peter Verkhovensky told me you were intelligent. Nicholas Stavrogin also told me about you. [SHATOV *turns away.*] In any case, here is my idea. In my opinion, and I think that you will agree with me, our country isn't sufficiently known. So I thought it would be worth while to gather in a single book all the significant events our newspapers have reported in several years. Such a book would automatically *be* Russia. If you would only help me... I need someone highly competent, and of course your work would be paid for.

||SHATOV: It's an interesting idea, even intelligent.... It deserves thinking about....Yes, it does.

LISA [*delighted*]: If the book sells, we shall share the profits. You would provide the outline and the work, and I the initial idea and the necessary funds.

SHATOV: But what makes you think that I can do this work? Why I rather than someone else?

LISA: Well, what I heard of you made me like you. Will you accept?

SHATOV: Maybe. Yes. Can you leave me your newspapers? I shall think about it.

LISA [*claps her hands with joy*]: Oh! How happy I am! How proud I shall be when the book comes out! || [*All this time she has been looking around her.*] By the way, doesn't Captain Lebyatkin live here?

GRIGORIEV: Yes, of course. I thought I told you so. Are you interested in him?

LISA: In him? Yes, but not only.... In any case, he is interested in me ... [*She looks at* GRIGORIEV.] He wrote me a letter with a poem in it, and he says that he has things to tell me. I didn't understand it at all. [*To* SHATOV] What do you think of him?

SHATOV: He's a drunkard and a dishonest man.

LISA: But I have heard that he lives with his sister.

SHATOV: Yes.

LISA: It is said that he bullies her. [SHATOV *looks at her fixedly without answering.*] But people say so many things, after all. I shall ask Nicholas Stavrogin, who knows her well, who knows her even very well, according to what I have heard ... [SHATOV *keeps on staring at her. With a sudden outburst of enthusiasm*] Oh, listen, I want to see her at once. I must see her in the flesh. Please help me. I really must.

SHATOV [*goes and picks up the newspapers*]: Take back your newspapers. I cannot accept this work.

LISA: Why not? Have I hurt you?

SHATOV: That's not it. You mustn't count on me for this chore, that's all.

LISA: What chore? This job is not imaginary. I want to do it.

SHATOV: Yes. You had better go home now.

GRIGORIEV [*affectionately*]: Yes. Please go home. Shatov will think about it. I shall come and see you and keep you informed. [LISA *looks at them, whimpers, then goes off in a hurry.*]

SHATOV: It was a pretext. She wanted to see Maria Timofeyevna, and I haven't sunk low enough to play a part in such a comedy. [MARIA TIMOFEYEVNA *has come in behind him. She is holding a roll in her hand.*]

MARIA: Good day, Shatoushka!

[GRIGORIEV *bows.* SHATOV *goes towards* MARIA TIMOFEYEVNA *and takes her arm. She walks towards the table in the centre, and places her roll on the table, pulls out a drawer, and takes out a deck of cards without paying any attention to* GRIGORIEV.] MARIA [*shuffling the cards*]: I was fed up with staying alone in my room.

SHATOV: I am pleased to see you.

MARIA: I am too. That man ... [*She points to* GRIGORIEV.] I don't know him. Let us honour all visitors! Yes, I always enjoy talking with you, even though you are always dishevelled. You live like a monk; let me comb your hair.

[*She takes a little comb from her pocket.*]

SHATOV [*laughing*]: But I have no comb.

[MARIA TIMOFEYEVNA *combs his hair.*]

MARIA: Really? Well, later on, when my Prince comes back, I'll give you mine. [*She makes a parting, steps back to judge the impression it makes, and puts the comb in her pocket.*] Shall I tell you, Shatoushka? [*She sits down and begins to play solitaire.*] You are intelligent and yet you are bored. After all, you are all bored. I can't understand anyone being bored. Being sad doesn't amount to being bored. *I* am sad, but I enjoy myself hugely.

SHATOV: Even when your brother is here?

MARIA: You mean my lackey? He is my brother, to be sure,

but, above all, he is my lackey, I order him about: 'Lebyatkin, water!' He goes and gets it. Sometimes I make the mistake of laughing at him, and when he is drunk he beats me. [*She goes on playing solitaire.*]

SHATOV [to GRIGORIEV]: That is true. She treats him like a lackey. He beats her, but she is not afraid of him. Besides, she hasn't the slightest notion of time – she forgets everything that has just happened. [GRIGORIEV *points towards her.*] No, I can talk in her presence; she has already forgotten us because very soon she stops listening and falls back into her daydreams. Do you see that roll? Probably she has nibbled it only once since this morning and won't finish it until tomorrow.

[MARIA TIMOFEYEVNA *picks up the roll without ceasing to look at her cards, but she holds it in her hand without biting into it. During the course of the conversation she puts it down on the table again.*]

MARIA: A move, a wicked man, a betrayal, a deathbed.... Why, these are all lies! If people can lie, why can't cards also? [*She scatters them over the table and gets up.*] Everyone lies except the Mother of God! [*She smiles as she looks at her feet.*]

SHATOV: The Mother of God?

MARIA: Why, yes, the Mother of God, nature, great mother earth! She is good and true. Do you remember what is written, Shatoushka? 'When you have wet the earth with your tears to the depth of a foot, then you will take joy in everything.' That's why I weep so often, Shatoushka. There is no harm in these tears. All tears are tears of joy or promises of joy. [*Her face is bathed in tears. She puts her hands on* SHATOV*'s shoulders.*] Shatoushka, is it true that your wife left you?

SHATOV: It is true. She forsook me.

MARIA [*caressing his face*]: Don't be angry. I too am grieving. I had a dream, you know. He returned. He, my Prince, returned, and called me in a sweet voice: 'My dear one,' he said, 'my dear one, come and join me.' And I was happy. I kept repeating: 'He loves me, he loves me.'

SHATOV: Perhaps he will really come.

MARIA: Oh, no, it was only a dream! My Prince will not come. I shall remain alone. Oh, my dear friend, why don't you ever question me about anything?

SHATOV: Because I know that you will never tell me anything.

MARIA: No, oh, no, I won't tell anything! They can kill me, they can burn me alive, but I won't tell anything. They'll never know anything!

SHATOV: See!

MARIA: Yet if you who are so kindhearted asked me, then perhaps. . . . Why don't you ask me? Ask me, ask properly, Shatoushka, and I shall tell you. Beg me to talk, Shatoushka. And I shall talk, I shall talk. . . .

[SHATOV *says nothing and* MARIA TIMOFEYEVNA *faces him with her face bathed in tears. Then a fracas and oaths are heard at the door.*]

SHATOV: Here is your brother. Go back to your room or he will beat you again.

MARIA [*bursting out laughing*]: Oh, it's my lackey? Well, what does it matter? We'll send him to the kitchen. [*But* SHATOV *draws her towards the door upstage.*] Don't worry, Shatoushka, don't worry. If my Prince comes back, he will defend me.

[LEBYATKIN *comes in and slams the door.* MARIA TIMOFEYEVNA *remains upstage with a frozen smile of scorn on her face.*]

LEBYATKIN [*singing drunkenly*]:

I have come to tell you
That the sun is up,
That the woods are swooning
Under his ardent kisses.

Who goes there? Friend or foe? [*To* MARIA TIMOFEYEVNA] You get back in your room!

SHATOV: Leave your sister alone.

LEBYATKIN [*bowing to* GRIGORIEV]: Retired Captain Ignatius Lebyatkin, in the service of the whole world and of his friends, just so long as they are faithful friends! Oh, the swine! And, first of all, I want you all to know that I am in love with Lisa Drozdov. She is a star and a horsewoman. In short, a star on horseback. And *I* am a man of honour.

SHATOV: Who sells his sister.

LEBYATKIN [*shouting*]: What? The same old calumny! Do you know that I could shame you with a single word?

SHATOV: Say the word.

LEBYATKIN: You think I wouldn't dare.

SHATOV: You may be a captain, but you are a coward. And you would be afraid of your master.

LEBYATKIN: He is provoking me, and you are a witness to it, sir! Well, do you know whose wife this woman is?

[GRIGORIEV *steps forward.*]

SHATOV: Whose? You won't dare say.

LEBYATKIN: She is.... She is...

[MARIA TIMOFEYEVNA *steps forward, her mouth open and speechless.*]

BLACKOUT

THE NARRATOR: Whose wife was that wretched cripple? Was it true that Dasha had been dishonoured, and by whom? And who had seduced Shatov's wife? Well, we shall be told! Indeed, just as the climate of our little city had become so tense, a newcomer came with a flaming torch which blew up everything and stripped everyone naked. And, take my word for it, seeing one's fellow citizens naked is generally a painful experience. So the son of the humanist, the offspring of the liberal Stepan Trofimovich, Peter Verkhovensky, to call him by name, popped up at the moment when he was least expected.

SCENE FOUR

At Varvara Stavrogin's. GRIGORIEV *and* STEPAN TROFIMOVICH.

STEPAN: Ah, my friend, everything is about to be decided. If Dasha accepts, I shall be a married man next Sunday, and that's not funny. But since my very dear Varvara Stavrogin asked me to come today and settle everything, I shall obey her. Didn't I behave badly towards her?

GRIGORIEV: No, not at all. You were simply taken by surprise.

STEPAN: Yes, I did. When I think of that generous and compassionate woman, so indulgent to all my petty foibles! I am a spoiled child with all the selfishness of a child and none of the innocence. She has been taking care of me for twenty years. And I, at the very moment when she is receiving these dreadful anonymous letters . . .

GRIGORIEV: Anonymous letters?

STEPAN: Yes, just imagine: she is told that Nicholas has given his property to Lebyatkin. That Nicholas is a monster. Poor Lisa! But you are in love with her, I know.

GRIGORIEV: How dare you?

STEPAN: All right, all right, forget it. Maurice Nicolaevich is in love with her too, don't forget. Poor man, I wouldn't want to be in his place. But, then, mine isn't much easier. || In any case, however ashamed of myself I am, I wrote to Dasha.

GRIGORIEV: Good Lord! What did you tell her?

STEPAN: Well . . . I wrote to Nicholas too.

GRIGORIEV: Are you crazy?

STEPAN: But my intention was noble. After all, just imagine that something really took place in Switzerland, or that there was a beginning, a little beginning, or even a very little beginning of something. I had to question their hearts first of all. I wanted them to know that I knew, so that they would feel freer. I acted through noble motives.

GRIGORIEV: But it was utterly stupid!

STEPAN: Yes, yes, it was foolish. But how else could I behave? Everything is open and above-board now. I wrote to my son, too. And yet I don't care! I'll marry Dasha even if I am just covering up the sins of others.

GRIGORIEV: Don't say that.

STEPAN: Oh, if only next Sunday would never come! It would be easy for God to perform a miracle and to cross one Sunday off the calendar. If only to prove his power to the atheists once and for all! How I love her! How I've loved her for twenty years! Can she really think for a minute that I am getting married because of fear, or poverty? I am doing it for her alone.

GRIGORIEV: Of whom are you talking?

STEPAN: Why, of Varvara, of course. She is the only woman I have adored for the last twenty years. [ALEXEY YEGOROVICH *comes in, escorting* SHATOV.] Ah, here is our quick-tempered friend. You have come to see your sister, I suppose . . .

SHATOV: No. I have been summoned by Varvara Stavrogin for a matter in which I am involved. That is the way, I believe, that the police word it when they issue a summons.

STEPAN: No, she meant just what she said, although I don't know what the business is, nor whether you are involved. In any case, our very dear Varvara is at Mass. As for Dasha, she is in her room. Do you want me to send for her?

SHATOV: No.

STEPAN: All right. That is probably better, after all. The later, the better. You probably know Varvara's plans for her?

SHATOV: Yes.

STEPAN: Good, good! In that case, let's say no more about it, let's say no more about it. Of course, I can imagine that you were surprised. I was myself. So suddenly . . .

SHATOV: Shut up.

STEPAN: All right. Be polite, my dear Shatov, at least today. Yes, be patient with me. My heart is heavy.

[VARVARA STAVROGIN *and* PRASCOVYA DROZDOV *enter, escorted by* MAURICE NICOLAEVICH.]

PRASCOVYA: What a scandal! And Lisa mixed up in all that!

VARVARA [*ringing for a servant*]: Be quiet! What do you call a scandal? That poor girl has lost her reason. Be a little charitable, my dear Prascovya!

STEPAN: What? What happened?

VARVARA: Nothing. A poor crippled girl threw herself at

my feet as we were leaving Mass and kissed my hand. [ALEXEY YEGOROVICH *comes in.*] Coffee . . . and don't unharness the horses.

PRASCOVYA: In front of everybody, and they all crowded around!

VARVARA: Of course, in front of everybody! Thank God the church was well filled! I gave her ten roubles and picked her up. Lisa insisted on taking her to her home. [LISA *enters, holding* MARIA TIMOFEYEVNA *by the hand.*]

LISA: No, I changed my mind. I thought that you would all be pleased to know Maria Timofeyevna better.

MARIA: How beautiful it is! [*She perceives* SHATOV.] What, you are here, Shatoushka! What are you doing in high society?

VARVARA [*to* SHATOV]: Do you know this woman?

SHATOV: Yes.

VARVARA: Who is she?

SHATOV: See for yourself.

[*She looks with anguish at* MARIA TIMOFEYEVNA. ALEXEY YEGOROVICH *comes in with coffee on a tray.*]

VARVARA [*to* MARIA TIMOFEYEVNA]: You were cold a moment ago, my dear. Drink this coffee – it will warm you up.

MARIA [*smiling*]: Yes. Oh, I had forgotten to give you back the shawl you lent me.

VARVARA: Keep it. It is yours. Sit down and drink your coffee. Don't be afraid.

STEPAN: *Chère amie* –

VARVARA: Oh, you, be quiet. The situation is bad enough without your making it any worse! Alexey, ask Dasha to come down.

PRASCOVYA: Lisa, we must leave now. This doesn't concern you. We have no further contact with this house.

VARVARA: You have gone a little too far, Prascovya. Thank God that there's no one but friends here to hear you.

PRASCOVYA: If they are friends, so much the better. But *I* am not afraid of public opinion. You are the one who, despite all your pride, trembles at the thought of what people will say. You are the one who is afraid of the truth.

VARVARA: What truth, Prascovya?

PRASCOVYA: This truth.

[*She points at* MARIA TIMOFEYEVNA, *who, seeing a finger pointing at her, giggles and fidgets.* VARVARA *stands up, white in the face, and mutters something that is not heard.* DASHA *enters upstage, and no one sees her but* STEPAN TROFIMOVICH.]

STEPAN [*after making signals intended to attract* VARVARA STAVROGIN'*s attention*]: Here is Dasha.

MARIA: Oh! How beautiful she is! Well, Shatoushka, your sister doesn't look like you at all.

VARVARA [*to* DASHA]: Do you know this person?

DASHA: I've never seen her. But I suppose she is Lebyatkin's sister.

MARIA: Yes, he is my brother. But, above all, he is my lackey. I didn't know you either, dearie. And yet I wanted very much to meet you, especially after my lackey told me that you had given him money. Now I am happy – you are charming. . . . Yes, charming, I tell you.

VARVARA: What money is she talking about?

DASHA: Nicholas Stavrogin had asked me in Switzerland to hand over a certain sum to Maria Lebyatkin.

VARVARA: Nicholas?

DASHA: Nicholas himself.

VARVARA [*after a silence*]: All right. Since he did so without mentioning it to me, he must have had reasons for doing so. But in the future I shall ask you to be more careful. That Lebyatkin has not a good reputation.

MARIA: Oh, no! And if he comes, you must send him to the kitchen. That's his place. You can give him coffee if you wish. But I hold him in utter contempt.

ALEXEY YEGOROVICH [*coming in*]: A certain Mr Lebyatkin is very insistent about being announced.

MAURICE: Allow me to say, madame, that he is not the kind of man to be received in good society.

VARVARA: Yet I am going to receive him. [*To* ALEXEY YEGOROVICH] Tell him to come up. [ALEXEY YEGOROVICH *leaves*.] Since you must know, I received anonymous letters informing me that my son is a monster and warning me against a crippled woman destined to play a large part in my life. I want to get to the bottom of the matter.

PRASCOVYA: I, too, have received those letters. And you know what they say about this woman and Nicholas . . .

VARVARA: I know.

[LEBYATKIN *comes in, titillated without being quite drunk. He goes towards* VARVARA STAVROGIN.]

LEBYATKIN: I have come, madame –

VARVARA: Sit down in that chair, sir. You can be heard just as well from there. [*He wheels about and goes and sits down.*] Now, will you introduce yourself?

LEBYATKIN [*rising*]: Captain Lebyatkin. I have come, madame –

VARVARA: Is this person your sister?

LEBYATKIN: Yes, madame. She eluded my vigilance for . . . I wouldn't want you to think that I was saying anything bad about my sister, but . . . [*He taps his forehead with his finger.*]

VARVARA: Did this misfortune happen long ago?

LEBYATKIN: On a certain day, madame, yes, a certain day.

... I have come to thank you for having taken her in. Here are twenty roubles. [*He goes towards her as the others all bestir themselves as if to protect* VARVARA STAVROGIN.]

VARVARA: Why, you must be mad, my man.

LEBYATKIN: No, madame. Rich is your dwelling and poor is the dwelling of the Lebyatkins, but Maria my sister, née Lebyatkin, the nameless Maria would not have accepted from anyone but you the ten roubles you gave her. From you, madame, and from you alone she will accept anything. But while she accepts with one hand, she gives with the other to one of your charities.

VARVARA: That is done through my porter, sir, and you may do so as you leave. I beg you therefore to put your money away and not to wave it in my face. I shall thank you also to sit down again. Now explain yourself and tell me why your sister can accept anything from me.

LEBYATKIN: Madame, that is a secret that I shall carry to the grave with me.

VARVARA: Why?

LEBYATKIN: May I ask you a question openly, in the Russian manner, from the depths of my heart?

VARVARA: I am listening.

LEBYATKIN: Is it possible to die just because of too noble a soul?

VARVARA: That is a question I have never asked myself.

LEBYATKIN: Really never? Well, if that's the way it is ... [*He strikes his chest vigorously.*] Be silent, heart; there is no hope!

[MARIA TIMOFEYEVNA *bursts out laughing.*]

VARVARA: Stop talking in conundrums, sir, and answer my question. Why can she accept anything from me?

LEBYATKIN: Why? Oh, madame, every day for millennia the whole of nature has been asking the Creator 'Why?'

and we are still awaiting the reply. Is Captain Lebyatkin to be the only one to answer? Would that be fair? I should like to be named Paul and yet I am named Ignatius. Why? I am a poet, with the soul of a poet, and yet I live in a pigsty. Why?

VARVARA: You are expressing yourself bombastically, and I look upon that as insolent.

LEBYATKIN: No, madame, not insolent. I am just an infinitesimal insect, but the insect does not complain. A man is sometimes forced to put up with the dishonour of his family rather than to speak the truth. So Lebyatkin will not complain; he will not say one word too many. You must, madame, admit his greatness of soul!

[ALEXEY YEGOROVICH *comes in, showing great emotion.*]

ALEXEY YEGOROVICH: Nicholas Stavrogin has come.

[*All turn towards the door. Hasty steps are heard and* PETER VERKHOVENSKY *enters.*]

STEPAN: But . . .

PRASCOVYA: But it's . . .

PETER: Greetings, Varvara Stavrogin.

STEPAN: Peter! Why, it's Peter, my son! [*He rushes up and embraces* PETER.]

PETER: All right. All right. Don't get excited. [*He breaks away.*] Just imagine, I rush in expecting to find Nicholas Stavrogin. He left me a half-hour ago at Kirilov's and asked me to meet him here. He will be here any minute, and I am happy to announce this good news.

STEPAN: But I haven't seen you for ten years.

PETER [*moving from one person to another in the room*]: All the more reason for not going all to pieces. Behave yourself! Oh, Lisa, how happy I am! And your esteemed mother hasn't forgotten me? How are your legs? Dear Varvara Stavrogin, I had told my father, but naturally he forgot . . .

STEPAN: *Mon enfant, quelle joie!*

PETER: Yes, you love me. But leave me alone. Ah! Here is Nicholas!

[STAVROGIN *enters.*]

VARVARA: Nicholas! [*At the tone of her voice,* STAVROGIN *stops dead.*] I beg you to tell me at once, before you take even one step, whether it is true that this woman here is your legitimate wife.

[STAVROGIN *stares at her, smiles, then walks towards her and kisses her hand. With the same calm stare he walks towards* MARIA TIMOFEYEVNA. MARIA *gets up with an expression of painful delight on her face.*]

STAVROGIN [*with extraordinary gentleness and affection*]: You must not stay here.

MARIA: May I, here and now, kneel down before you?

STAVROGIN [*smiling*]: No, you may not. I am not your brother or your fiancé or your husband, am I? Take my arm. With your permission, I shall take you home to your brother. [*She casts a frightened look towards* LEBYATKIN.] Fear nothing. Now that I am here, he will not touch you.

MARIA: Oh, I fear nothing. At last you have come. Lebyatkin, call for the carriage.

[LEBYATKIN *leaves.* STAVROGIN *gives his arm to* MARIA TIMOFEYEVNA, *who takes it with a radiant expression on her face. But as she walks she stumbles and would fall but for* STAVROGIN *holding her. He leads her towards the exit, showing her great consideration, amid an absolute silence.* LISA, *who has risen from her chair, sits down again with a shudder of disgust. As soon as they have left, everyone stirs.*]

VARVARA [*to* PRASCOVYA DROZDOV]: Well, did you hear what he just said?

PRASCOVYA: Of course. Of course! But why didn't he answer you?

PETER: Why, he couldn't, I assure you!

VARVARA [*suddenly looking at him*]: Why not? What do you know about it?

PETER: I know all about it. But the story was too long for Nicholas to relate just now. I can tell it to you, for I saw it all.

VARVARA: If you give me your word of honour that what you say will not hurt Nicholas in any way ...

PETER: Quite the contrary! He will even be grateful to me for having spoken. You see, we were together in St Petersburg five years ago and Nicholas was leading – how shall I put it? – an ironic life. Yes, that's the word. He was bored then, but did not want to fall into despair. Hence he did nothing and went out with anyone at all. Through nobility of soul, you might say, like a man above all that sort of thing. In short, he spent his time with knaves. Thus it is that he knew that Lebyatkin, a fool and parasite. He and his sister were living in abject poverty. One day in a cabaret someone insulted that lame girl. Nicholas got up, seized the insulter by the collar, and with a single blow threw him out. That's all.

||VARVARA: What do you mean, 'that's all'?

PETER: Yes, that's where it all started. The lame girl fell in love with her Knight, who spoke two sentences to her. People made fun of her. Nicholas was the only one who didn't laugh and treated her with respect.||

STEPAN: Why, that is very chivalrous.

||PETER: Yes, you see, my father feels the same way that the lame girl did. Kirilov, on the other hand, did not.

VARVARA: Why not?

PETER: He used to say to Nicholas: 'It's because you treat her like a duchess that she is losing all self-possession.'

LISA: And what did the Knight reply?

PETER: 'Kirilov,' he said, 'you think I am making fun of her, but you are wrong. I respect her, for she is worth more than all of us.'

STEPAN: Sublime! And even, you might say, chivalrous. . . ||

PETER: Yes, chivalrous. Unfortunately, the lame girl eventually came to imagine that Nicholas was her fiancé. Finally, when Nicholas had to leave Petersburg, he arranged to leave behind an annual allowance for the lame girl.

LISA: Why that?

PETER: I don't know. A whim perhaps – the kind a man indulges in when he is prematurely tired of existence. Kirilov, on the other hand, claimed that it was the fancy of a blasé young man who wanted to see how far he could lead a half-crazy cripple. But I am sure that's not true.

VARVARA [*in a state of rapture*]: Why, of course not! It's just like Nicholas! It's just like me! Being carried away like that, blind generosity taking up the defence of anything weak, infirm, perhaps even unworthy . . . [*She looks at* STEPAN TROFIMOVICH] . . . protecting the creature for years on end. . . . Why, it's me all over again! Oh, I have been guilty towards Nicholas! As for that poor creature, it's very simple; I shall adopt her.

PETER: And you will be doing right. For her brother persecutes her. He got it into his head that he had a right to dispose of her allowance. Not only does he take everything she has, not only does he beat her and take her money, but he drinks it all up, he insults her benefactor, threatens to drag him before the law if the allowance is not paid to him directly. In fact, he considers Nicholas's gift as if it were a sort of tribute.

LISA: A tribute for what?

PETER: Well, how should I know? He talks of his sister's

honour, of his family. But honour is a vague word, isn't it? Very vague.

SHATOV: Is it a vague word, really? [*All look at him.*] Dasha, is it a vague word to you? [DASHA *looks at him.*] Answer me.

DASHA: No, brother, honour exists.

[STAVROGIN *enters.* VARVARA *rises and goes rapidly towards him.*]

VARVARA: Oh, Nicholas, will you forgive me?

STAVROGIN: I am the one to be forgiven, Mother. I should have explained to you. But I was sure that Peter Verkhovensky would inform you.

VARVARA: Yes, he did. And I am happy.... You were chivalrous.

STEPAN: Sublime is the word.

STAVROGIN: Chivalrous, indeed! So that's how you see it? I suppose I owe this compliment to Peter Verkhovensky. And you must believe him, Mother. He lies only in exceptional circumstances. [PETER VERKHOVENSKY *and* STAVROGIN *look at each other and smile.*] Good, but I beg your forgiveness once more for my attitude. [*In a harsh, crisp voice*] In any case, the subject is closed now. There's no point in bringing it up again. [LISA *bursts out with a hysterical laugh.*]

STAVROGIN: Good day, Lisa. I hope you are well.

LISA: Please forgive me. I believe you know Maurice Nicolaevich. Good Lord, Maurice, how is it possible to be so tall?

MAURICE: I don't understand.

LISA: Oh, nothing ... I was just thinking.... Supposing that I were lame, you would lead me through the streets, you would be chivalrous, wouldn't you? You would be devoted to me?

MAURICE: Most certainly, Lisa. But why talk of such a misfortune?

LISA: Most certainly you would be chivalrous. Well, you so tall and I crippled and deformed, we'd make a ridiculous couple.

[VARVARA STAVROGIN *and* PRASCOVYA DROZDOV *go towards* LISA. *But* STAVROGIN *turns and goes towards* DASHA.]

STAVROGIN: I've heard of your marriage, Dasha, and I want to congratulate you. [DASHA *turns her head away.*] My congratulations are sincere.

DASHA: I know it.

PETER: Why these congratulations? Am I to assume that there is some good news?

PRASCOVYA: Yes, Dasha is getting married.

PETER: Why, it's wonderful! Accept my congratulations too. But you have lost your bet. You told me in Switzerland that you would never get married. Decidedly, it's an epidemic. Do you know that my father is getting married too?

STEPAN: Peter!

PETER: Well, didn't you write me so? To be sure, you weren't very clear. First you declare yourself to be delighted and then you ask me to save you; you tell me that the girl is a pure diamond, but that you must get married to cover sins committed in Switzerland; you ask my consent – what a topsy-turvy world this is! – and you beg me to save you from this marriage. [*To the others, laughing*] What on earth could he mean? But that's the way his generation is – big words and vague ideas! [*He seems suddenly to become aware of the effect of his words.*] Well, what's the matter? . . . It looks as if I've dropped a brick. . . .

VARVARA [*stepping towards him with flushed face*]: Did Stepan Trofimovich write you that in so many words?

PETER: Yes, here is his letter. It is long, like all of his letters. I never read them all the way through, I must confess. Besides, he doesn't care, for he writes them especially for posterity. But there's no harm in what he says.

VARVARA: Nicholas, was it Stepan Trofimovich who informed you of this marriage? In the same manner, I suppose?

STAVROGIN: He did write me, in fact, but a very noble letter.

VARVARA: That's enough! [*She turns towards* STEPAN TROFIMOVICH.] Stepan Trofimovich, I expect a great service of you. I expect you to leave this house and never appear in my presence again.

[STEPAN TROFIMOVICH *steps towards her and bows with great dignity, then goes over towards* DASHA.]

STEPAN: Dasha, forgive me for all this. I thank you for having accepted.

DASHA: I forgive you, Stepan Trofimovich. I feel nothing but affection and esteem for you. You, at least, continue to respect me.

PETER [*striking his forehead*]: Now I understand! Why, he meant with Dasha! Forgive me, Dasha. I didn't know. If only my father had had the sense to tell me instead of indulging in innuendo!

STEPAN [*looking at him*]: Is it possible that you knew nothing! Is it possible that you are not putting on an act?

PETER: Well, you see, Varvara Stavrogin, he's not only an aged child, he's also an aged naughty child. How could I have understood? A sin committed in Switzerland! Just try to make out what he means!

STAVROGIN: Be quiet, Peter, your father acted nobly. And

you have insulted Dasha, whom all of us here respect. [SHATOV *gets up and walks towards* STAVROGIN, *who smiles at him but ceases to smile when* SHATOV *is close to him. Everyone stares at them. Silence. Then* SHATOV *slaps him as hard as he can.* VARVARA *screams.* STAVROGIN *seizes* SHATOV *by the shoulders, then lets him go and puts his hands behind his back.* SHATOV *backs up as* STAVROGIN *stares at him.* STAVROGIN *smiles, bows, and leaves.*]

LISA: Maurice, come here. Give me your hand! [*Pointing to* STAVROGIN] You see that man? You won't see any better. Maurice, before all let me declare that I have agreed to be your wife!

MAURICE: Are you sure, Lisa, are you sure?

LISA [*staring at the door through which* STAVROGIN *has gone out, her face bathed in tears*]: Yes, yes, I am sure!

CURTAIN

SECOND PART

SCENE FIVE

At Varvara Stavrogin's. ALEXEY YEGOROVICH *holds on his arm a coat, a scarf, and a hat. In front of him* STAVROGIN *is dressing to go out.* PETER VERKHOVENSKY, *looking sullen, is near the table.*

STAVROGIN [*to* PETER]: And if you speak to me again like that, you will feel my cane.

PETER: There was nothing insulting in my proposition. If you really think of marrying Lisa . . .

STAVROGIN: . . . you can free me from the only obstacle separating me from her. I know it, but don't say it again. I'd rather not have to use my cane on you. My gloves, Alexey.

ALEXEY: It is raining, sir. At what time shall I expect you?

STAVROGIN: At two o'clock at the latest.

ALEXEY: Very well, sir. [STAVROGIN *takes his cane and is about to leave by the small door.*] May God bless you, sir. But only if you are planning a good deed.

STAVROGIN: What?

ALEXEY: May God bless you. But only if you are planning a good deed.

STAVROGIN [*after a silence and with his hand on* ALEXEY'*s arm*]: My good Alexey, I remember the time when you used to carry me in your arms.

[*He goes out.* ALEXEY *leaves by a door upstage.* PETER VERKHOVENSKY *looks around him, then goes over and ransacks the drawer of a writing-desk. He takes out some letters and reads them.* STEPAN TROFIMOVICH *enters.* PETER *hides the letters.*]

STEPAN: Alexey Yegorovich told me you were here, son.

PETER: Why, what are you doing in this house? I thought you had been driven out.

STEPAN: I came to get the last of my things, and I am going to leave without hope of returning and without recriminations.

PETER: Oh, you'll come back! A parasite is always a parasite.

STEPAN: I don't like the way you talk to me.

||PETER: You have always said that truth was paramount. The truth is that you pretended to be in love with Varvara Petrovna and that she pretended not to see that you were in love with her. As a reward for such silliness, she was keeping you. Hence you are a parasite. I advised her yesterday to put you in a suitable home.

STEPAN: You spoke to her about me?

PETER: Yes, she told me that tomorrow she would have a conversation with you to settle everything. The truth is that she wants to see you squirm once more. She showed me your letters. How I laughed – good Lord, how I laughed!

STEPAN: You laughed. Have you no heart! || Do you know what a father is?

PETER: You taught me what a father is. You never provided for me. I wasn't even weaned when you shipped me off to Berlin by the post. Like a parcel.

STEPAN: Wretch! Although I sent you by the post, my heart continued to bleed!

PETER: Mere words!

STEPAN: Are you or aren't you my son, monster?

PETER: You must know better than I. To be sure, fathers are inclined to have illusions about such things.

STEPAN: Shut up!

PETER: I will not. And don't whimper. You are a patriotic, snivelling, whimpering old woman. Besides, all Russia whimpers. Fortunately, we are going to change all that.

STEPAN: Who is 'we'?

PETER: Why, we normal men. We are going to remake the world. We are the saviours.

STEPAN: Is it possible that anyone like you aims to offer himself up to men in the place of Christ? But just look at yourself!

PETER: Don't shout. We shall destroy everything. We'll not leave a stone standing, and then we'll begin all over again. Then there will be true equality. You preached equality, didn't you? Well, you shall have it! And I bet that you won't recognize it.

STEPAN: I shall not recognize it if it looks like you. No, it was not of such things that we used to dream! I don't understand anything any more. I have given up understanding.

PETER: All that comes from your sick old nerves. *You* made speeches. *We* act. What are you complaining about, scatterbrained old man?

STEPAN: How can you be so insensitive?

PETER: I followed your teachings. According to you, the thing to do was to treat injustice harshly and to be sure of one's rights, to go ever forwards towards the future! Well, that's where we're going, and we shall strike hard. A tooth for a tooth, as in the Gospels!

STEPAN: You poor fellow, it's not in the Gospels!

PETER: The devil take it! I have never read that confounded

book. Nor any other book. What's the use? What matters is progress.

STEPAN: No, you're crazy! Shakespeare and Hugo don't stand in the way of progress. Quite the contrary, I assure you!

PETER: Don't get excited! Hugo is an old pair of buttocks. As for Shakespeare, our peasants working in the fields don't need him. They need shoes instead. They will be given them as soon as everything is destroyed.

STEPAN [*trying to be ironic*]: And when will this be?

PETER: In May. In June everyone will be making shoes. [STEPAN TROFIMOVICH *falls into a chair, crushed.*] Rejoice, ancestor, for your ideas are going to be put into practice.

STEPAN: They are not my ideas. You want to destroy everything; you don't want to leave a single stone standing. But *I* wanted people to love one another.

PETER: No need for love! Science will take its place.

STEPAN: But that will be boring.

PETER: Why should it be boring? That's an aristocratic idea. When men are equal, they are not bored. They don't have a good time either. Nothing matters and everything is on the same plane. When we have justice plus science, then both love and boredom will be done away with. People will forget.

STEPAN: No man will ever be willing to forget his love.

PETER: Again you're indulging in words. Just remember, ancestor, that you forgot; you got married three times.

STEPAN: Twice. And after a long interval.

PETER: Long or short, people forget. Consequently, the sooner they forget, the better. Oh, but you get on my nerves, never knowing what you want! *I* know what I want. Half the heads will have to be cut off. Those that remain will be taught to drink.

STEPAN: It is easier to cut off heads than to have ideas.

PETER: What ideas? Ideas are nonsense. Nonsense has to be suppressed to achieve justice. Nonsense was good enough for old men like you. A man has to choose. If you believe in God, you are forced to talk nonsense. If you don't believe in Him and yet refuse to admit that everything must be razed, you will still talk nonsense. You're all in the same boat, and consequently you can't keep yourselves from talking nonsense. *I* say that men must act. I'll destroy everything and others will construct. No more reform and no more improvement. The more things are improved and reformed, the worse it is. The sooner people begin to destroy, the better it is. Let's begin by destroying. What happens afterwards doesn't concern us. The rest is nonsense, nonsense!

STEPAN [*rushing out of the room, terrified*]: He's mad, he's mad....

[PETER VERKHOVENSKY *laughs uproariously*.]

BLACKOUT

THE NARRATOR: Well, so much for that! I have forgotten to tell you two facts. The first is that the Lebyatkins had mysteriously moved while Stavrogin was bedridden and had settled in a little house in the suburbs. The second is that a convicted murderer had escaped and was prowling among us. As a result, rich people did not go out at night.

The street at night. STAVROGIN *is walking in the dark, unaware that* FEDKA *is following him.*

SCENE SIX

The common room of the Filipov lodging-house in Epiphany Street. KIRILOV *is on all fours to retrieve a ball that has rolled under a piece of furniture. While he is in that position,* STAVROGIN *opens the door.* KIRILOV, *with the ball in his hand, gets up as he sees him come in.*

STAVROGIN: You are playing ball?

KIRILOV: I bought it in Hamburg to throw it up and catch it; nothing strengthens the back like that. Besides, I play with the landlady's boy.

STAVROGIN: Do you like children?

KIRILOV: Yes.

STAVROGIN: Why?

KIRILOV: I like life. You want tea?

STAVROGIN: Yes.

KIRILOV: Sit down. What do you want of me?

STAVROGIN: A service. Read this letter. It is a challenge from the son of Gaganov, whose ear I bit some time back. [KIRILOV *reads it and then places it on the table and looks at* STAVROGIN.] ||Yes, he has already written me several times to insult me. In the beginning I answered to assure him that if he was still suffering from the insult I had done his father, I was ready to offer him every apology. I insisted that my deed had not been premeditated and that I was ill at the time. Instead of calming him, this seemed to irritate him even more, if I can believe what he said about me. Today I am handed this letter. || Have you read what he says at the end?

KIRILOV: Yes, he speaks of a 'face I'd like to smack'.

STAVROGIN: That's it. Hence I have to fight him, although I don't want to. I have come to ask you to be my second.

KIRILOV: I'll go. What should I say?

STAVROGIN: Begin by repeating my apologies for the offence done to his father. Tell him that I am ready to forget his insults if only he will cease writing me this kind of letter, especially with such vulgar expressions.

KIRILOV: He won't accept. It's clear that he wants to fight you and kill you.

STAVROGIN: I know it.

KIRILOV: Good. Tell me your conditions for the duel.

STAVROGIN: I want everything to be over tomorrow. Go and see him tomorrow morning at nine o'clock. We can be on the field at about two. ||The weapon will be the pistol. The barriers will be ten yards apart. Each of us shall take his stand ten paces from his barrier. At the signal we shall walk towards each other. Each may shoot as he walks. We shall shoot three times. That's all.

KIRILOV: Ten yards between the barriers isn't much.

STAVROGIN: Twelve, if you prefer. But no more.|| Have you pistols?

KIRILOV: Yes. You want to see them?

STAVROGIN: Certainly.

[KIRILOV *kneels down in front of a travelling bag and takes out a pistol case, which he places on the table in front of* STAVROGIN.]

KIRILOV: I also have a revolver I bought in America. [*He shows it to him.*]

STAVROGIN: You have many guns. And very handsome ones.

KIRILOV: They are my sole wealth.

[STAVROGIN *looks at him fixedly, then closes the pistol case without ceasing to look at him.*]

STAVROGIN [*with a slight hesitation*]: Are you still firm in your intention?

KIRILOV [*immediately and with a most natural manner*]: Yes.

STAVROGIN: I mean in regard to suicide.

KIRILOV: I understood what you meant. Yes, I have the same intentions.

STAVROGIN: Ah! And when will it be?

KIRILOV: Soon.

STAVROGIN: You seem very happy.

KIRILOV: I am.

STAVROGIN: I understand that. I have sometimes thought of it. Just imagine that you have committed a crime, or, rather, a particularly cowardly, shameful deed. Well, a bullet in the head and everything ceases to exist! What does shame matter then!

KIRILOV: That's not why I am happy.

STAVROGIN: Why, then?

KIRILOV: Have you ever looked at the leaf of a tree?

STAVROGIN: Yes.

KIRILOV: Green and shiny, with all its veins visible in the sunlight? Isn't it wonderful? Yes, a leaf justifies everything. Human beings, birth and death – everything one does is good.

STAVROGIN: And even if . . . [*He stops.*]

KIRILOV: Well?

STAVROGIN: If a man harms one of those children you love . . . a little girl, for instance. . . . If he dishonours her, is that good too?

KIRILOV [*staring at him in silence*]: Did you do that? [STAVROGIN *shakes his head oddly in silence.*] If a man commits such a crime, that is good too. And if someone splits open the head of a man who dishonoured a child or if, on the other hand, he is forgiven, all that is good.

When we know that once and for all, then we are happy.

STAVROGIN: When did you discover that you were happy?

KIRILOV: Last Wednesday. During the night. At two thirty-five. [STAVROGIN *rises suddenly.*]

STAVROGIN: Was it you who lighted the lamp in front of the icon?

KIRILOV: It was I.

||STAVROGIN: Do you pray?

KIRILOV: Constantly. Do you see that spider? I watch her and am grateful to her for climbing. That's my way of praying.

STAVROGIN: Do you believe in a future life?

KIRILOV: Not in eternal life in the future. But in eternal life here below.

STAVROGIN: Here below?

KIRILOV: Yes. At certain moments. Such a joy that one would die if it lasted more than five seconds.||

[STAVROGIN *looks at him with a sort of comtempt.*]

STAVROGIN: And you claim not to believe in God!

KIRILOV [*quite simply*]: Stavrogin, I beg you not to use irony in talking to me. Just remember what you were for me, the part you played in my life.

STAVROGIN: It's late. Be in time tomorrow morning at Gaganov's. Remember ... nine o'clock.

KIRILOV: I am punctual. I can wake up when I want to. When I go to bed I tell myself 'Seven o'clock', and I awaken at seven o'clock.

STAVROGIN: That is a very valuable trait.

KIRILOV: Yes.

STAVROGIN: Go and sleep. But first tell Shatov that I want to see him.

KIRILOV: Just a minute. [*He takes a stick from the corner and knocks on the side wall.*] There, he'll come now. But what about you; won't you sleep? You are duelling tomorrow.

STAVROGIN: Even when I am tired, my hand never trembles.

KIRILOV: That's a valuable trait. Good night.

[SHATOV *appears in the doorway upstage.* KIRILOV *smiles at him and leaves by the side door.* SHATOV *stares at* STAVROGIN *and then enters slowly.*]

SHATOV: How you worried me! Why were you so slow in coming?

STAVROGIN: Were you so sure that I would come?

SHATOV: I couldn't imagine that you would forsake me. I can't get along without you. Just remember the part you played in my life.

STAVROGIN: Then why did you strike me? [SHATOV *says nothing.*] Was it because of my affair with your wife?

SHATOV: No.

STAVROGIN: Because of the rumour that started about your sister and me?

SHATOV: I don't think so.

STAVROGIN: Good. It hardly matters anyway. As I don't know where I'll be tomorrow evening, I came merely to give you a warning and to ask you a service. Here is the warning: you may be murdered.

SHATOV: Murdered?

STAVROGIN: By Peter Verkhovensky's group.

||SHATOV: I knew it. But how did you find out?

STAVROGIN: I belong to their group. Like you.

SHATOV: You, Stavrogin, are a member of their society? You joined up with those vain and idiotic flunkeys? How could you? Is that worthy of Nicholas Stavrogin?

STAVROGIN: Forgive me, but you ought to get out of the habit of looking upon me as the Tsar of all the Russias and yourself as just a speck of dust.

SHATOV: Oh, don't talk to me that way! You know very well that they are knaves and flunkeys and that you don't belong among them!

STAVROGIN: Indubitably they are knaves. But what does that matter? To tell the truth, I don't belong altogether to their society. Whenever I helped them in the past, I did so as a dabbler and because I had nothing better to do.

SHATOV: Is it possible to do such things as a dabbler?

STAVROGIN: People sometimes get married as dabblers, or have children and commit crimes as dabblers! But, speaking of crimes, you are the one running the risk of being killed. Not I. At least not by them. ||

SHATOV: They have nothing against me. I joined their organization. But my ideas changed when I was in America. I told them so when I got back. I was very fair in telling them that we disagreed on all points. That's my privilege, the right of my conscience. I will not accept –

STAVROGIN: Don't shout. [KIRILOV *comes in, picks up the pistol case, and leaves.*] Verkhovensky won't hesitate to liquidate you if he gets the idea that you might compromise their organization.

SHATOV: They make me laugh. Their organization doesn't even exist.

STAVROGIN: I suppose in fact that it's all a figment of Verkhovensky's brain. ||The others think he is a delegate of an international organization and so they follow him. But he has the talent to make them accept his myth. That's the way you form a group. And then some day, starting from the first group, he may succeed in creating the international organization. ||

SHATOV: That insect, that poor fool, that idiot who doesn't know anything about Russia!

STAVROGIN: It is true that such people don't know anything about Russia. But, after all, they know only a little less about it than we do. Besides, even an idiot can shoot a revolver. Which is why I came to warn you.

SHATOV: Thank you. And I thank you particularly for doing so after I struck you.

STAVROGIN: Not at all. I return good for evil. [*He laughs.*] Don't worry, I am a Christian. Or, rather, I should be if I believed in God. But . . . [*He gets up.*] . . . there is no hare.

SHATOV: No hare?

STAVROGIN: Yes, to make jugged hare you need a hare. To believe in God you need a God. [*He laughs again, but icily this time.*]

SHATOV [*greatly excited*]: Don't blaspheme like that! Don't laugh! And get rid of that pose; take on a normal human manner. Speak simply and humanly, if only for once in your life! And remember what you used to say before I left for America.

STAVROGIN: I don't remember.

SHATOV: I'll tell you. It's high time for someone to tell you the truth about yourself, to strike you if need be and remind you of what you are. Do you recall the time when you used to tell me that the Russian people alone would save the universe in the name of a new God? Do you remember your words: 'A Russian atheist is an impossibility'? You didn't say then that the hare doesn't exist.

STAVROGIN: I seem indeed to remember our conversations.

SHATOV: The devil take your conversations! There *were* no conversations! There was simply a master proclaiming great truths and a disciple rising from the dead. I was the disciple and you were the master.

STAVROGIN: Great truths, really?

SHATOV: Yes, really. || Wasn't it you who told me that if it were mathematically proven that truth stood apart from Christ, you would rather be with Christ than with truth? ||Wasn't it you who used to say that the blind life-force driving a nation in search of its god is greater than reason and science and that it alone determines good and evil, and that hence the Russian nation, if it is to march in the van of humanity, must follow its Christ? || I believed you. The seed germinated in me, and –

STAVROGIN: I am happy for your sake.

SHATOV: Drop that pose! Drop it at once or I'll. . . . Yes, you told me all that. And at the same time you used to say just the opposite to Kirilov, as I learned from him in America. You were pouring falsehood and negation into his heart. You were driving his reason towards madness. Have you seen him since? Have you contemplated your handiwork?

STAVROGIN: Let me point out to you that Kirilov himself has just told me he was utterly happy.

SHATOV: That is not what I am asking you. How could you tell him one thing and me the opposite?

STAVROGIN: Probably I was trying, in both cases, to persuade myself.

SHATOV [*with a note of despair*]: And now you are an atheist and don't believe what you taught me?

STAVROGIN: And you?

SHATOV: I believe in Russia, in its orthodoxy, in the body of Christ. . . . I believe that the second coming will take place in Russia. I believe –

STAVROGIN: And in God?

SHATOV: I . . . I *shall* believe in God one day.

STAVROGIN: That's just it. You don't believe. Besides, can anyone be intelligent and still believe? It's an impossibility.

SHATOV: No, I didn't say that I didn't believe. We are all dead or half dead and incapable of believing. But men must rise up, and you must be the first. I am the only one who knows your intelligence, your genius, the breadth of your culture, of your conceptions. In the whole world each generation produces but a handful of superior men, two or three. You are one of them. You are the only one, yes, the only one who can raise the flag.

STAVROGIN: I note that everyone at the moment wants to thrust a flag into my hands. Verkhovensky, too, would like me to bear their flag. But he does so because he admires what he calls my 'extraordinary aptitude for crime'. What should I make of all this?

SHATOV: I know that you are also a monster. That you have been heard to assert that you saw no difference between any bestial act and a great deed of sacrifice. ||It is even said that in St Petersburg you belonged to a secret society that indulged in revolting debauches.|| They say, they also say – but I can't believe this – that you used to attract children to your house to defile them.... [STAVROGIN *suddenly rises.*] Answer. Tell the truth. Nicholas Stavrogin cannot lie to Shatov, who struck him in the face. Did you do that? If you did it, you could not bear the flag and I should understand your despair and your helplessness.

STAVROGIN: Enough. Such questions are unseemly. [*He stares at* SHATOV.] What does it matter anyway? *I* am interested only in more ordinary questions. Such as: should one live or should one destroy oneself?

SHATOV: Like Kirilov?

STAVROGIN [*with a sort of melancholy*]: Like Kirilov. But he will go all the way. He is a Christ.

SHATOV: And you.... Would you be capable of destroying yourself?

STAVROGIN [*painfully*]: I ought to! I ought to! But I am afraid of being too cowardly. Perhaps I shall do so tomorrow. Perhaps never. That is the question ... the only question I ask myself.

SHATOV [*hurling himself at* STAVROGIN *and seizing him by the shoulder*]: That's what you are seeking. You are seeking punishment. Kiss the ground, water it with your tears, beg for mercy!

STAVROGIN: Hands off, Shatov. [*He holds him at a distance, and with an expression of pain*] Just remember: I could have killed you the other day and I folded my hands behind my back. So don't persecute me.

SHATOV [*leaping backwards*]: Oh, why am I condemned to believe in you and to love you? I cannot tear you from my heart, Nicholas Stavrogin. I shall kiss your footprints on the floor when you have left.

STAVROGIN [*with the same expression*]: I regret to have to tell you, but I cannot love you, Shatov.

SHATOV: I know it. You cannot love anyone because you are a man without roots and without faith. ||Only men who have roots in the soil can love and believe and build. The others destroy. And you destroy everything without intending to, and you are even drawn to idiots like Verkhovensky who want to destroy for their own comfort, simply because it is easier to destroy than not to destroy.|| But I shall lead you back to your former way. You will find peace and I shall cease being alone with what you have taught me.

STAVROGIN: Thank you for your good intentions. But until you have a chance to help me find the hare, you could do me the more modest service I came to ask of you.

SHATOV: And what is it?

STAVROGIN: If I happened to disappear in one way or another, I should like you to take care of my wife.

SHATOV: Your wife? Are you married?

STAVROGIN: Yes, to Maria Timofeyevna. ||I know that you have considerable influence over her. You are the only one who can . . .||

SHATOV: So it is true that you married her?

STAVROGIN: Four years ago in Petersburg.

SHATOV: Were you obliged to marry her?

STAVROGIN: Obliged? No.

SHATOV: Have you a child by her?

STAVROGIN: She has never had a child and couldn't have one. Maria Timofeyevna is still a virgin. But I ask you simply to take care of her.

[SHATOV, *dazed, watches him leaving. Then he runs after him.*]

SHATOV: Ah! I understand. I know you. I know you. You married her to punish yourself for a dreadful crime. [STAVROGIN *makes a gesture of impatience.*] Listen, listen, go and see Tihon.

STAVROGIN: Who is Tihon?

SHATOV: A former bishop who has retired here to the Monastery of St Euthymia. He will help you.

STAVROGIN [*staring at him*]: Who in this world could help me? Not even you, Shatov. And I'll never ask you anything again. Good night.

SCENE SEVEN

A bridge at night. STAVROGIN *is walking in another direction under the rain, having opened his umbrella.* FEDKA *pops up behind him.*

FEDKA: Might I, sir, take advantage of your umbrella?
[STAVROGIN *stops. He and* FEDKA *face each other under the umbrella.*]

STAVROGIN: Who are you?

FEDKA: No one important. But you, you are Mr Stavrogin, a noble lord!

STAVROGIN: You are Fedka, the convict!

FEDKA: I am not a convict any more. I was sent up for life, to be sure. But I found time dragging and changed my status.

STAVROGIN: What are you doing here?

FEDKA: Nothing. I need a passport. In Russia it's impossible to make a move without a passport. Fortunately, a man you know, Peter Verkhovensky, promised me one. Meanwhile, I was lying in wait for you in the hope that Your Grace would give me three roubles.

STAVROGIN: Who gave you the order to lie in wait for me?

FEDKA: No one, no one! Although Peter Verkhovensky told me incidentally that perhaps with my talents I could do a service for Your Grace, in certain circumstances, by ridding you of people who are in your way. As he told me also that you would go over this bridge to see a certain party on the other side of the river, I have been waiting for you the past three nights. You see that I deserve my three roubles.

STAVROGIN: Good. Listen. I like to be understood. You will not receive a kopeck from me and I neither have nor shall have need of you. If I ever find you in my way again on this bridge or anywhere else, I'll bind you and hand you over to the police.

FEDKA: Yes, but *I* need you.

STAVROGIN: Begone or I'll strike you.

FEDKA: Please take into consideration, sir, that I am a poor defenceless orphan and that it is raining!

STAVROGIN: I give you my word of honour that if I meet you again, I'll bind you up.

FEDKA: I'll wait for you anyhow. You never know!

[*He disappears.* STAVROGIN *stares in his direction for a moment.*]

BLACKOUT

SCENE EIGHT

The Lebyatkins' dwelling. STAVROGIN *is already in the room.* LEBYATKIN *is relieving him of his umbrella.*

LEBYATKIN: What frightful weather! Oh, you are all wet. [*He pushes up an armchair.*] I beg you, I beg you. [*He straightens up.*] Ah, you are looking at this room. You see, I live like a monk. Abstinence, solitude, poverty, according to the three vows of the knights of old.

STAVROGIN: Do you think the knights of old took such vows?

LEBYATKIN: I don't know. I am perhaps confusing things.

STAVROGIN: You are certainly confusing things. I hope that you haven't been drinking.

LEBYATKIN: Hardly at all.

STAVROGIN: I asked you not to get drunk.

LEBYATKIN: Yes. Odd request!

STAVROGIN: Where is Maria Timofeyevna?

LEBYATKIN: In the next room.

STAVROGIN: Is she sleeping?

LEBYATKIN: Oh, no, she is telling her fortune. She is expecting you. As soon as she heard the news, she got all dressed up.

STAVROGIN: I shall see her in a moment. But first I have something to settle with you!

LEBYATKIN: I hope so. So many things have piled up in my heart. I should like to be able to talk freely with you, as I used to do. Oh, you have played such a great part in my life. And now I am treated so cruelly.

STAVROGIN: I see, Captain, that you haven't changed at all in the past four years. [*He stares at him silently.*] ||So they are right, those who claim that the second half of a human life is determined by the habits acquired during the first half.

LEBYATKIN: Oh! what sublime words! Why, the enigma of life is solved! And yet|| I insist that I am casting my skin like a serpent. Besides, I have written my will.

STAVROGIN: That's odd. To bequeath what and to whom?

LEBYATKIN: I want to leave my skeleton to the medical students.

||STAVROGIN: And you hope for payment during your lifetime?

LEBYATKIN: And why not? You see, I read the biography of an American in the newspapers. He bequeathed his huge fortune to scientific foundations, his skeleton to the medical students of the city, and his skin to be made into a drum on which the American national anthem would be beaten night and day. But, alas, we are merely pygmies in comparison to the Americans and their boldness of thought. If I tried to do the same, I'd be accused of being a socialist and my skin would be confiscated. Consequently, I had to be satisfied with the students. I want to leave them my skeleton on condition that a label will be stuck to my skull saying: 'A repentant freethinker'. ||

STAVROGIN: So you know that you are in danger of death.

LEBYATKIN [*giving a start*]: No, not at all. What do you mean? What a joke!

STAVROGIN: Didn't you write a letter to the governor to denounce Verkhovensky's group, to which you belong nevertheless?

LEBYATKIN: I don't belong to their group. I agreed to hand out proclamations, but only to do a service, as it were. I wrote to the governor to explain something of the sort to him. But if Verkhovensky really thinks.... Oh, I must get to St Petersburg. That's why I was waiting for you. Anyway, my dear benefactor, I need money to go there.

STAVROGIN: You will have nothing from me. I have already given you too much.

LEBYATKIN: That's true. But *I* accepted the shame of it.

STAVROGIN: What shame is there in the fact that your sister is my legitimate wife?

LEBYATKIN: But the marriage is kept secret! It is kept secret and there is a fatal mystery about it! I receive money from you – all right, that's normal. Then I am asked: 'Why do you receive that money?' I am bound by my word and cannot answer, thus wronging my sister and the honour of my family.

STAVROGIN: I have come to tell you that I am going to

make up for that outrage done to your noble family. Tomorrow, probably, I shall announce our marriage officially. Hence the question of the family dishonour will be settled. And likewise, of course, the question of the allowance that I shan't have to pay you.

LEBYATKIN [*panic-stricken*]: But it's not possible. You can't make this marriage public. She is half crazy.

STAVROGIN: I'll take care of that.

LEBYATKIN: What will your mother say? You will have to take your wife into your house.

STAVROGIN: That doesn't concern you.

LEBYATKIN: But what shall *I* become? You are casting me off like an old worn-out shoe.

STAVROGIN: Yes, like an old shoe. That's the correct expression. Now call Maria Timofeyevna.

[LEBYATKIN *goes out and brings back* MARIA TIMOFEYEVNA, *who stands in the middle of the room.*]

STAVROGIN [*to* LEBYATKIN]: Leave now. No, not that way. I'm afraid you would listen to us. I mean outside.

LEBYATKIN: But it's raining.

STAVROGIN: Take my umbrella.

LEBYATKIN [*bewildered*]: Your umbrella – really, am I worthy of that honour?

STAVROGIN: Every man is worthy of an umbrella.

LEBYATKIN: Yes, yes, of course, that's a part of the rights of man! [*He goes out.*]

MARIA: May I kiss your hand?

STAVROGIN: No. Not yet.

MARIA: All right. Sit down in the light so that I can see you.

[*To reach the armchair,* STAVROGIN *walks towards her. She crouches down with her arm raised as if to protect herself, an expression of fright on her face.* STAVROGIN *stops.*]

STAVROGIN: I frightened you. Forgive me.

MARIA: Never mind. No, I was wrong.

[STAVROGIN *sits down in the light.* MARIA TIMOFEYEVNA *screams.*]

STAVROGIN [*with a touch of impatience*]: What's the matter?

MARIA: Nothing. Suddenly I didn't recognize you. It seemed to me that you were someone else. What are you holding in your hand?

STAVROGIN: What hand?

MARIA: Your right hand. It's a knife?

STAVROGIN: But look, my hand is empty.

MARIA: Yes. Last night I saw in a dream a man who looked like my Prince, but it wasn't he. He was coming towards me with a knife. Ah! [*She screams.*] Are you the murderer from my dream or my Prince?

STAVROGIN: You are not dreaming. Calm yourself.

MARIA: If you are my Prince, why don't you kiss me? To be sure, he never kissed me. But he was affectionate. I don't feel anything affectionate in you. On the other hand, there's something stirring in you that threatens me. He called me his dove. He gave me a ring. He said: 'Look at it in the evening and I'll come to you in your sleep.'

STAVROGIN: Where is the ring?

MARIA: My brother drank it up. And now I am alone at night. Every night ... [*She weeps.*]

STAVROGIN: Don't weep, Maria Timofeyevna. From now on we shall live together.

[*She stares at him fixedly.*]

MARIA: Yes, your voice is soft now. And I recall. I know why you are telling me we shall live together. The other day in the carriage you told me that our marriage would be made public. But I'm afraid of that, too.

STAVROGIN: Why?

MARIA: I'll never know how to handle guests. I don't suit you at all. I know, there are lackeys. But I saw your family – all those ladies – at your house. They are the ones I don't suit.

STAVROGIN: Did they do anything to hurt you?

MARIA: Hurt? Not at all. I was watching you all. There you were, getting excited and bickering. You don't even know how to laugh freely when you are together. So much money and so little joy! It's dreadful. No, I wasn't hurt. But I was sad. It seemed to me that you were ashamed of me. Yes, you were ashamed, and that morning you began to be more remote. Your very face changed. My Prince went away, and I was left with the man who scorned me, who perhaps hated me. No more kind words – just impatience, anger, the knife . . . [*She gets up, trembling.*]

STAVROGIN [*suddenly beside himself*]: Enough! You are mad, mad!

MARIA [*in a meek, little voice*]: Please, Prince, go outside and come back in.

STAVROGIN [*still trembling and impatiently*]: Come back in? Why come back in?

MARIA: So that I'll know who you are. For those five years I was waiting for him to come, I constantly imagined the way he would come in. Go outside and come back in as if you had just returned from a long absence, and then perhaps I'll recognize you.

STAVROGIN: Be quiet. Now, listen carefully. I want all your attention. Tomorrow, if I'm still alive, I shall make our marriage public. We shall not live in my house. We shall go to Switzerland, to the mountains. We shall spend our whole life in that gloomy, deserted spot. That is how I see things.

MARIA: Yes, yes, you want to die, you are already burying

yourself. But when you come to want to live again, you will want to get rid of me. No matter how!

STAVROGIN: No, I shall not leave that place; I'll not leave you. Why do you talk to me like this?

MARIA: Because now I have recognized you and I know that you are not my Prince. *He* would not be ashamed of me. He would not hide me in the mountains. He would show me to everyone – yes, even to that young lady who couldn't take her eyes off me the other day. No, you look very much like my Prince, but it's all over. . . . I have seen through you. *You* want to make an impression on that young lady. You covet her.

STAVROGIN: Will you listen to me? Cease this madness!

MARIA: *He* never told me I was mad. He was a Prince, an eagle. He could fall at the feet of God if he wanted to, and not fall at the feet of God if he didn't want to. As for you, Shatov slapped you. You are a lackey too.

STAVROGIN [*taking her by the arm*]: Look at me. Recognize me. I am your husband.

MARIA: Let go of me, impostor. I don't fear your knife. *He* would have defended me against the whole world. *You* want my death because I am in your way.

STAVROGIN: What have you said, you wretch! What have you said?

[*He flings her backwards. She falls and he rushes towards the door. She stumbles after him. But* LEBYATKIN *suddenly appears and holds her down while she screams.*]

MARIA: Assassin! Anathema! Assassin!

BLACKOUT

SCENE NINE

The bridge. STAVROGIN *is walking rapidly while muttering to himself. When he has gone beyond the middle of the bridge,* FEDKA *pops up behind him.* STAVROGIN *turns around suddenly, seizes him by the neck, and pins him face downwards on the ground, without seeming to make an effort. Then he lets go of him. At once* FEDKA *is on his feet with a broad short knife in his hand.*

STAVROGIN: Put away that knife! [FEDKA *hides the knife.* STAVROGIN *turns his back and continues walking.* FEDKA *follows him. A long walk. The bridge has now been replaced by a long, deserted street.*] I almost broke your neck, I was so angry.

FEDKA: You are strong, Excellency. The soul is weak, but the body is vigorous. Your sins must be great.

STAVROGIN [*laughing*]: So you've gone in for preaching? Yet I have heard that you robbed a church last week.

FEDKA: To tell the truth, I had gone in to pray. And then it occurred to me that Divine Grace had led me there and that I should take advantage of it because God was willing to give me a little help.

STAVROGIN: You slaughtered the watchman too.

FEDKA: You might say we cleaned out the church together. But in the morning, down by the river, we fell to disputing as to who should carry the big bag. And then I sinned.

STAVROGIN: Superb. Go on slaughtering and robbing!

FEDKA: That's what little Verkhovensky told me. I'm quite willing. There are plenty of opportunities. Why, at Captain Lebyatkin's, where you went this evening . . .

STAVROGIN [*suddenly stopping*]: Well?

FEDKA: Now, don't hit me again! I mean that that drunkard leaves the door open every night, he is so drunk. Anyone could go in and kill everyone in the house, both brother and sister.

STAVROGIN: Did you go in?

FEDKA: Yes.

STAVROGIN: Why didn't you kill everybody?

FEDKA: I made a little calculation.

STAVROGIN: What?

FEDKA: I could steal a hundred and fifty roubles after having killed him – after having killed *them,* I mean. But if I am to believe little Verkhovensky, I could get fifteen hundred roubles from you for the same work. So ... [STAVROGIN *looks at him in silence.*] I am turning to you as to a brother or father. ||Nobody will ever know anything about it, not even young Verkhovensky.|| But I need to know whether you want me to do it: just give me the word or a little down payment. [STAVROGIN *begins to laugh as he looks at him.*] Now, wouldn't you like to give me the three roubles I asked you for earlier?

[STAVROGIN, *still laughing, takes notes out of his pocket and drops them on the ground one by one.* FEDKA *picks them up uttering 'ahs' which go on after the light has dimmed to* BLACKOUT.]

THE NARRATOR: The man who kills, or plans to kill, or lets others be killed, often wants to die himself. He is a comrade of death. Perhaps that is what Stavrogin's laugh meant. But it is not certain that Fedka understood it thus.

BLACKOUT

||SCENE TEN*

The Forest of Brykovo. It is wet and windy. The trees are bare, the ground is soaking wet. On the stage are two barriers. In front of one of them, STAVROGIN, *wearing a light coat and a white beaver hat, and in front of the other,* GAGANOV – *thirty-three years old, tall, fat, well fed, blond. In the middle are the seconds,* MAURICE NICOLAEVICH *on Gaganov's side and* KIRILOV. *The opponents already hold their pistols.*

KIRILOV: And now for the last time I propose a reconciliation. I say this only to observe the rules; it is my duty as a second.

MAURICE: I wholeheartedly approve Mr Kirilov's words. The idea that there can be no reconciliation on the field is merely a prejudice which we can leave to the French. Besides, there's no sense in this duel, since Mr Stavrogin is ready to offer his apologies again.

STAVROGIN: I confirm once more my proposal to offer every possible apology.

GAGANOV: But this is unbearable! We're not going to go through the same comedy again. [*To* MAURICE NICOLAEVICH] If you are my second and not my enemy, explain to this man ... [*He points at him with his pistol.*] ... that his concessions only aggravate the insult. He always seems to consider that my offensive remarks can't touch him and that there is no shame in dodging me. He insults me constantly, I tell you, and you are only irritating me so that I'll miss him.

KIRILOV: That's enough. I beg you to follow my orders.

*The whole scene of the duel was cut in production.

Back to your places. [*The opponents go back to their places behind the barriers, almost in the wings.*] One, two, three, go.

[*The opponents walk towards each other.* GAGANOV *shoots, stands still for a moment, and, seeing that he missed* STAVROGIN, *goes and takes his place at his barrier.* STAVROGIN *walks towards him and shoots above* GAGANOV. *Then he takes out a pocket handkerchief and wraps it around his little finger.*]

KIRILOV: Are you wounded?

STAVROGIN: The bullet scraped me.

KIRILOV: If your opponent does not declare himself satisfied, your duel must continue.

GAGANOV: I declare that that man shot intentionally in the air. It's one more insult.

STAVROGIN: I give you my word of honour that I have no intention of insulting you. I shot in the air for reasons that concern no one but me.

MAURICE: It seems to me, however, that if one of the opponents declares in advance that he will shoot in the air, the duel cannot go on.

STAVROGIN: I never said that I would shoot in the air each time. You don't know how I shall shoot the second time.

GAGANOV: I repeat that he did it on purpose. But I want to shoot a second time, according to my right.

KIRILOV [*wryly*]: It is in fact your right.

MAURICE: Since that is the way it is, the duel goes on.

[*They start in the same way.* GAGANOV *reaches the barrier and takes aim for a long time at* STAVROGIN, *who stands waiting with his arms at his sides.* GAGANOV*'s hand trembles.*]

KIRILOV: You are aiming too long. Shoot. Shoot quickly.

[GAGANOV *shoots.* STAVROGIN*'s hat flies off.* KIRILOV *picks it up and gives it to* STAVROGIN. *Together they examine the hat.*]

MAURICE: Your turn to shoot. Don't keep your opponent waiting.

[STAVROGIN *looks at* GAGANOV *and shoots his pistol upwards.* GAGANOV, *mad with rage, runs offstage.* MAURICE NICOLAEVICH *follows him.*]

KIRILOV: Why didn't you kill him? You have insulted him even more seriously.

STAVROGIN: What should I have done?

KIRILOV: Either not provoke him to a duel or else kill him.

STAVROGIN: I didn't want to kill him. But if I had not provoked him, he would have slapped me in public.

KIRILOV: Well, then, you would have been slapped!

STAVROGIN: I'm beginning to feel as if I didn't understand. Why does everybody expect of me what no one expects of anyone else? Why must I endure what no one endures and accept burdens that no one could carry?

KIRILOV: You go out of your way to seek those burdens, Stavrogin.

STAVROGIN: Ah! [*A pause.*] You noticed that?

KIRILOV: Yes.

STAVROGIN: Is it as obvious as that?

KIRILOV: Yes.

[*Silence.* STAVROGIN *puts on his hat and arranges it carefully. He resumes his distant manner, then looks at* KIRILOV.]

STAVROGIN [*slowly*]: One tires of burdens, Kirilov. It is not my fault that that idiot missed me.

BLACKOUT

SCENE ELEVEN

At Varvara Stavrogin's. STAVROGIN, *in the centre, is asleep bolt upright on the sofa, with a bandage on his finger. He scarcely seems to be breathing. His face is pale and severe, as if petrified, and he is frowning.*

DASHA *comes in and rushes to him, stops, and stares at him. She makes the sign of the cross over him. He opens his eyes and remains motionless, staring fixedly at the same point in front of him.*

DASHA: Are you wounded?

STAVROGIN [*looking at her*]: No.

DASHA: Did you draw blood?

STAVROGIN: No, I killed no one and, above all, no one killed me, as you see. The duel took place quite stupidly. I shot in the air and Gaganov missed me. I have no luck. But I am tired and should like to be alone.

DASHA: All right. I shall stop seeing you, since you constantly run away from me. I know that at the end I'll find you.

STAVROGIN: At the end?

DASHA: Yes. When all is over, call me and I'll come.

[*He looks at her and seems to wake up completely.*]

STAVROGIN [*in a natural manner*]: I am so vile and cowardly, Dasha, that I believe I shall actually call you at the very end. And you, despite all your prudence, will come running in fact. But, tell me, will you come, whatever the end is? [DASHA *is silent.*] Even if in the meantime I have committed the worst of crimes?

DASHA [*looking at him*]: Are you going to bring about your wife's death?

STAVROGIN: No. No. Neither hers nor anyone's. I don't

want to. Perhaps I shall bring about the death of the other one, the girl. . . . Perhaps I shall not be able to keep myself from doing so. Oh, leave me, Dasha. Why destroy yourself by following me? [*He gets up.*]

DASHA: I know that at the end I'll be alone with you, and I'm waiting for that moment, I pray for it.

STAVROGIN: So you pray?

DASHA: Yes. Ever since a certain day, I haven't ceased praying.

STAVROGIN: And suppose I don't call you? Suppose I take flight. . . .

DASHA: That can't be. You will call me.

STAVROGIN: There is great contempt in what you are saying.

DASHA: There is not only contempt.

STAVROGIN [*laughing*]: So, there *is* contempt. That doesn't matter. I don't want to cause your ruin.

DASHA: You won't cause my ruin. If I don't come with you, I shall become a nun and take care of the sick.

STAVROGIN: A nurse! That's it. That's it. You are interested in me just as a nurse would be. After all, that's probably what I need the most.

DASHA: Yes, you are ill.

STAVROGIN *suddenly takes a chair and flings it without apparent effort across the room.* DASHA *screams.* STAVROGIN *turns his back on her and goes and sits down. Then he talks quite naturally, as if nothing had happened.*]

STAVROGIN: You see, Dasha, I constantly have visions now. They're a kind of little demon. There is one, above all . . .

DASHA: You already told me about him. You are ill.

STAVROGIN: Last night he sat down very close to me and didn't leave me. He is stupid and insolent. And second-rate. Yes, second-rate. I am furious that my personal demon should be second-rate.

DASHA: You talk about him as if he really existed. Oh, may God save you from that.

STAVROGIN: No, no. I don't believe in the devil. Yet last night the demons came out of every swamp and swooped down upon me. Why, a little devil on the bridge offered to cut the throats of Lebyatkin and his sister, Maria Timofeyevna, to get rid of my marriage. He asked for a down payment of three roubles, but he calculated the cost of the operation at fifteen hundred roubles. He was a book-keeper devil.

DASHA: Are you sure he was a vision?

STAVROGIN: No, he was not a vision. It was Fedka, the escaped convict.

DASHA: What did you reply?

STAVROGIN: Why, nothing at all. To get rid of him, I gave him the three roubles and even more. [DASHA *exclaims.*] Yes. He must think I am in agreement. But don't let your kind heart worry. For him to act, I shall have to give him the order. Perhaps, after all, I shall give it!

DASHA [*clasping her hands*]: Good Lord, good Lord, why do you torment me like this?

STAVROGIN: Forgive me. It was only a joke. Besides, I've been like this since last night – I have a terrible impulse to laugh, to laugh without stopping, endlessly... [*He gives her a forced, hollow laugh.* DASHA *stretches out her hand towards him.*] I hear a carriage. It must be my mother.

DASHA: May God preserve you from your demons. Call me. I shall come.

STAVROGIN: Listen, Dasha. If I were to go and see Fedka and give him the order, would you come, would you come even after the crime?

DASHA [*in tears*]: Oh, Nicholas, Nicholas, I beg you, don't stay alone like this. . . . Go and see Tihon at the seminary; he will help you.

STAVROGIN: You too!

DASHA: Yes, Tihon. And afterwards I shall come. . . . I shall come . . . [*She flees, weeping.*]

STAVROGIN: Of course she'll come. With delight. [*With disgust*] Ah! . . .

||ALEXEY YEGOROVICH [*coming in*]:* Maurice Nicolaevich wishes to see you.

STAVROGIN: He? What can he . . . [*He has a smug smile.*] I'll see him.

[MAURICE NICOLAEVICH *enters and* ALEXEY YEGOROVICH *leaves.* MAURICE NICOLAEVICH *sees* STAVROGIN'*s smile and stops, as if he were about to wheel around and leave. But* STAVROGIN'*s expression changes, and, with a look of sincere surprise, he holds out his hand, which* MAURICE NICOLAEVICH *does not shake.* STAVROGIN *smiles again, but courteously this time.*]

STAVROGIN: Sit down.

[MAURICE NICOLAEVICH *sits on a chair and* STAVROGIN *at an angle on the sofa. For a minute* STAVROGIN *looks silently at his visitor, who seems to hesitate and then suddenly speaks.*]

MAURICE: If you can, marry Lisa Nicolayevna.

[STAVROGIN *stares at him without any change of expression.* MAURICE NICOLAEVICH *stares back.*]

STAVROGIN [*after a pause*]: If I am not wrong, Lisa Nicolayevna is your fiancée.

MAURICE: Yes, we are officially engaged.

*The scene between Maurice Nicolaevich and Stavrogin was cut in production

STAVROGIN: Have you had a quarrel?

MAURICE: No. She loves and esteems me, in her own words. And her words are the most precious thing in the world to me.

STAVROGIN: I can understand that.

MAURICE: I know that if you were to call her, though she stood at the altar in her wedding veil, she would forsake me and everyone else to follow you.

STAVROGIN: Are you sure of that?

MAURICE: Yes, she says she hates you, and she is sincere. But in reality she loves you insanely. And although she says she loves me, there are moments when she hates me cordially.

STAVROGIN: Yet I am surprised that you can dispose of Lisa Nicolayevna. Did she authorize you to do so?

MAURICE: You have just made a vulgar remark, a remark full of vengeance and scorn. But I'm not afraid to humiliate myself even more. No, I have no right, nor any authority. Lisa doesn't know what I am doing. Without her knowing it, I have come to tell you that you alone can make her happy and that you must take my place at the altar. Moreover, after saying this, I could never marry her. I could never live with myself.

STAVROGIN: If I married her, would you kill yourself after the ceremony?

MAURICE: No. Much later. Perhaps never...

STAVROGIN: You are saying that to set my mind at rest.

MAURICE: To set your mind at rest! A little blood more or less – what does that matter to you!

STAVROGIN [*after a pause*]: I assure you that I am deeply touched by your proposition. However, what makes you think that my feelings for Lisa are such that I want to marry her?

MAURICE [*rising suddenly*]: What? Don't you love her? Didn't you try to win her hand?

STAVROGIN: I can't ever talk to anyone of my feelings for a woman, except to the woman herself. Forgive me, but that's a quirk of my nature. However, I can tell you the truth as to everything else: I am married, and hence it is not possible for me to marry another woman or to try to win her hand, as you say. [MAURICE NICOLAEVICH *looks at him as if petrified, grows pale, and strikes the table violently with his fist.*]

MAURICE: If after such a confession you don't leave Lisa alone, I'll take a club and beat you to death like a dog. [*He leaps up and rushes out, at the door bumping into* PETER VERKHOVENSKY, *who is on the point of coming in.*] ||

PETER: Why, he's crazy! What did you do to him?

STAVROGIN [*laughing*]: Nothing. Besides, it doesn't concern you.

PETER: I am sure he came to offer you his fiancée. Eh? I am the one who indirectly pushed him into it, if you want to know. And if he refuses to give her to us, we'll take her ourselves, won't we? She's a juicy morsel.*

STAVROGIN: You still intend to help me take her, I see.

PETER: As soon as you decide to. We'll get rid of your responsibilities for you. It won't cost you anything.

STAVROGIN: Oh, yes it will. Fifteen hundred roubles.... By the way, what have you come for?

*After omitting the preceding scene, the following text was substituted for the last three lines:

ALEXEY [*coming in*]: Peter Verkhovensky insists on seeing you.

PETER [*following him closely*]: I have just met Maurice Nicolaevich. He wanted to give you his fiancée. I advised him to wait. Besides, we don't really need him; she is crazy to come. We'll go and get her ourselves, won't we? She's a juicy morsel.

PETER: What? Have you forgotten? What about our meeting? I have come to remind you that it takes place in an hour.

STAVROGIN: Oh, to be sure! Excellent idea. You couldn't have picked a more opportune moment. I feel like having a good time. What part am I supposed to play?

PETER: You are one of the members of the Central Committee and you know all about the whole secret organization.

STAVROGIN: What am I to do?

PETER: Just assume a mysterious look, that's all.

STAVROGIN: But there is no Central Committee?

PETER: Yes, there is. You and I.

STAVROGIN: In other words, you. And there is no organization?

PETER: There will be one if I can manage to organize those idiots into a group, to weld them into a single unit.

STAVROGIN: How will you go about it?

PETER: Well, to begin with, titles and functions – secretary, treasurer, president – you know the kind of thing! Then sentimentality. For them justice is a matter of sentimentality. Hence, they must be given plenty of opportunity to talk, especially the stupider ones. In any case, they are united by fear of opinion. That is the motivating force, the real cement. The thing they fear most of all is being taken for reactionaries. Consequently, they are obliged to be revolutionaries. They would be ashamed of thinking for themselves, of having an individual idea. As a result, they will think as I want them to.

STAVROGIN: Excellent programme! But I know a much better way of cementing this pretty group together. Force four members to kill the fifth on the pretext that he is a stool pigeon, and they will be bound by blood.

But how stupid I am – it's precisely your idea, isn't it, since you want to have Shatov killed?

PETER: I! Why . . . what makes you think of such a thing!

STAVROGIN: No, *I'm* not thinking of it. But *you* are. And if you want my opinion, it's not at all stupid. ||In order to bind men together, there is something stronger than sentimentality or fear of opinion; it is dishonour.|| The best way of attracting our fellow citizens and of sweeping them along with you is to preach publicly the right to dishonour.

PETER: Yes, I know it. Hurrah for dishonour and everybody will come to us; no one will want to lag behind. Ah, Stavrogin, you understand everything! You will be the leader and I'll be your secretary. We shall set sail on a noble ship. The masts will be of polished wood, the sails silken, and on the high stern we shall put Lisa Nicolayevna.

STAVROGIN: There are only two objections to that prophecy. The first is that I shall not be your leader –

PETER: You will; I'll explain to you.

STAVROGIN: The second is that I'll not help you kill Shatov to bind your idiots together. [*He laughs uproariously.*]

PETER [*bursting with wrath*]: I . . . I must go and tell Kirilov.

[*He rushes out. The moment he is gone,* STAVROGIN *ceases laughing and sits down on the sofa, silent and sinister-looking.*]

BLACKOUT

The street. PETER VERKHOVENSKY *is walking towards Kirilov's.*

THE NARRATOR [*suddenly appearing as* VERKHOVENSKY *disappears*]: At the same time that Peter Verkhovensky arrived, something began spreading over the town. Mysterious fires broke out; the number of thefts doubled. A second lieutenant who had got into the habit of lighting candles in his room in front of books expounding materialist ideas suddenly scratched and bit his commanding officer. A lady of the highest society began beating her children at fixed intervals and insulting the poor whenever she had an opportunity. And another wanted to practise free love with her husband. 'That's impossible,' she was told. 'What do you mean?' she exclaimed; 'we're free, aren't we?' We were free indeed, but of what?

SCENE TWELVE

KIRILOV, FEDKA, *and* PETER VERKHOVENSKY *in the living-room of the Filipov lodging-house. Shatov's room is dimly lighted.*

PETER [*to* FEDKA]: Mr Kirilov will hide you.

FEDKA: You are a vile little insect, but I'll obey you, I'll obey you. Just remember what you promised me.

PETER: Go and hide.

FEDKA: I'll obey. Just remember. [FEDKA *disappears.*]

KIRILOV [*as if noting a fact*]: He loathes you.

PETER: He doesn't have to like me; all he has to do is obey me. Sit down. I have something to say to you. I came to remind you of the agreement binding us.

KIRILOV: I am not bound by anything or to anything.

PETER [*giving a start*]: What, have you changed your mind?

KIRILOV: I have not changed my mind. But I act according to my own will. I am free.

PETER: All right, all right. I am willing to admit that it is your own free will, provided that your will hasn't changed. You get excited about a word. You have become very irritable of late.

KIRILOV: I am not irritable, but I don't like you. Yet I shall keep my word.

PETER: But it must be very clear between us. You still intend to kill yourself?

KIRILOV: Still.

PETER: Fine. Admit that no one is forcing you to it.

KIRILOV: You are expressing yourself stupidly.

PETER: All right, all right. I expressed myself very stupidly. Beyond a shadow of a doubt, no one can force you. Let me go on. You belonged to our organization and you confessed your plan to one of its members?

KIRILOV: I did not confess anything; I simply said what I would do.

PETER: Good, good. Indeed, there was no reason to confess anything. You simply made a statement. Fine.

KIRILOV: No, it's not fine. You're just talking. I made up my mind to kill myself because I want to. You saw that my suicide could help the organization. If you commit a crime here and the guilty are pursued, I blow out my brains, leaving a letter in which I declare that I am the guilty one. So you asked me to wait a while before killing myself. I answered that I would wait, since it didn't matter to me.

PETER: Good. But you gave your word to write the letter with my help and to wait for my orders. Only in this matter, of course, for in everything else you are free.

KIRILOV: I didn't give my word. I agreed because it was a matter of indifference to me.

PETER: If you wish. Do you still feel the same?

KIRILOV: Yes. Will it be soon?

PETER: In a few days.

KIRILOV [*rising as if reflecting*]: Of what should I declare myself guilty?

PETER: You'll know in time.

KIRILOV: Good. But don't forget this: I'll not help you in any way against Stavrogin.

PETER: All right, all right.

[SHATOV *enters from an inner room.* KIRILOV *sits down in a corner.*]

PETER: It's good of you to have come.

SHATOV: I don't need your approval.

PETER: You are wrong. In the fix you are in, you will need my help, and I have already used up considerable breath in your favour.

SHATOV: I don't have to answer to anyone. I am free.

PETER: Not altogether. Many things were entrusted to you. You have no right to break off without warning.

SHATOV: I sent a very clear letter.

PETER: We didn't understand it clearly. They say that you might denounce them now. I defended you.

SHATOV: Yes, just as there are lawyers who make a business of getting people hanged.

PETER: In any case, they have agreed now for you to be free if only you return the printing press and the papers. Where is the press?

SHATOV: In the forest. Near the Brykovo clearing. I buried everything in the ground.

PETER [*with a sort of smile*]: In the ground? Very good! Why, it's very good indeed!

[*There is a knock at the door. The plotters enter:* LIPUTIN, VIRGINSKY, SHIGALOV, LYAMSHIN, *and a defrocked seminarist. As they settle down, they are already talking.* SHATOV *and* KIRILOV *in a corner.*]

VIRGINSKY [*at the door*]: Ah! Here is Stavrogin.

LIPUTIN: He's just in time.

THE SEMINARIST: Gentlemen, I am not accustomed to waste my time. Since you were so kind as to invite me to this meeting, may I ask a question?

LIPUTIN: Go ahead, comrade, go ahead. Everyone here likes you since you played that practical joke on the woman distributing religious tracts by sticking obscene photographs in her Bibles.

THE SEMINARIST: It wasn't a practical joke. I did it out of conviction, being of the opinion that God must be destroyed.

LIPUTIN: Is that what they teach in the seminary?

THE SEMINARIST: No. In the seminary they suffer because of God. Consequently they hate him. In any case, here is my question: has the meeting begun or not?

SHIGALOV: Allow me to point out that we continue to talk aimlessly. Can the authorities tell us why we are here?

[*All look towards* VERKHOVENSKY, *who changes his position as if he were about to speak.*]

LIPUTIN [*in a hurry*]: Lyamshin, please sit down at the piano.

LYAMSHIN: What? Again! It's the same every time!

LIPUTIN: If you play, no one can hear us. Play, Lyamshin! For the cause!

VIRGINSKY: Why, yes, play, Lyamshin.

[LYAMSHIN *sits down at the piano and plays a waltz haphazardly. All look towards* VERKHOVENSKY, *who, far from speaking, has resumed his somnolent position.*]

LIPUTIN: Verkhovensky, have you no declaration to make?

PETER [*yawning*]: Absolutely none. But I should like a glass of cognac.

LIPUTIN: And you, Stavrogin?

STAVROGIN: No, thanks, I've given up drinking.

LIPUTIN: I'm not talking of cognac. I'm asking you if you want to speak.

STAVROGIN: Speak? What about? No.

[VIRGINSKY *gives the bottle of cognac to* PETER VERKHOVENSKY, *who drinks a great deal during the evening. But* SHIGALOV *rises, dull and sombre-looking, and lays on the table a thick notebook filled with fine writing, which all look at with fear.*]

SHIGALOV: I request the floor.

VIRGINSKY: You have it. Take it.

[LYAMSHIN *plays louder.*]

THE SEMINARIST: Please, Mr Lyamshin, but really we can't hear ourselves.

[LYAMSHIN *stops playing.*]

SHIGALOV: Gentlemen, in asking for your attention, I owe you a few preliminary explanations.

PETER: Lyamshin, pass me the scissors that are on the piano.

LYAMSHIN: Scissors? For what?

PETER: I forgot to cut my nails, I should have done so three days ago. Go on, Shigalov, go on; I'm not listening.

SHIGALOV: Having devoted myself wholeheartedly to studying the society of the future, I reached the conclusion that from the earliest times down to the present all creators of social systems simply indulged in nonsense. So I had to build my own system or organization. Here it is! [*He strikes the notebook.*] To tell the truth, my system is not completely finished. In its present state, however, it deserves discussion. For I shall have to explain to you also the contradiction to which it leads. Starting from unlimited freedom, I end up in fact with unlimited despotism.

VIRGINSKY: That will be hard to make the people swallow!

SHIGALOV: Yes. And yet – let me insist upon it – there is not and there cannot be any other solution to the social problem than mine. It may lead to despair, but there is no other way.

THE SEMINARIST: If I have understood properly, the agenda concerns Mr Shigalov's vast despair.

SHIGALOV: Your expression is more nearly correct than you think. Yes, I was brought smack up against despair. And yet there was no other way out but my solution. If you don't adopt it, you will do nothing worth while. And some day you'll come round to it.

THE SEMINARIST: I suggest voting to find out just how far Mr Shigalov's despair interests us and whether it is necessary for us to devote our meeting to the reading of his book.

VIRGINSKY: Let's vote! Let's vote!

LYAMSHIN: Yes, yes.

LIPUTIN: Gentlemen! Gentlemen! Let's not get excited. Shigalov is too modest. I have read his book. Certain of its conclusions are debatable. But he started from human nature as we now know it through science and he really solved the social problem.

THE SEMINARIST: Really?

LIPUTIN: Yes, indeed. He proposes dividing humanity into two unequal parts. About a tenth will have absolute freedom and unlimited authority over the other nine tenths, who will have to lose their personality and become like a flock of sheep. Kept in the state of complete submission of sheep, they will, on the other hand, achieve the state of innocence of sheep. In short, it will be Eden, except that men will have to work.

SHIGALOV: Yes. That's how I achieve equality. All men

are slaves and equal in their slavery. They can't be equal otherwise. Hence it is essential to level. For instance, the level of education and talent will be lowered. Since men of talent always tend to rise, Cicero's tongue will have to be torn out, Copernicus's eyes gouged out, and Shakespeare stoned. There is my system.

LIPUTIN: Yes, Mr Shigalov discovered that superior faculties are germs of inequality, hence of despotism. Consequently, as soon as a man is seen to have superior gifts, he is shot down or imprisoned. Even very handsome people are suspect in this regard and must be suppressed.

SHIGALOV: And even fools, if they are very notable fools, for they might lead others into the temptation of glorifying in their superiority, which is a germ of despotism. By these means, on the other hand, equality will be absolute.

THE SEMINARIST: But you have fallen into a contradiction. Such equality is despotism.

SHIGALOV: That's true, and that's what drives me to despair. But the contradiction disappears the moment you say that such despotism is equality.

PETER [*yawning*]: What nonsense!

LIPUTIN: Is it really nonsense? On the contrary, I find it very realistic.

PETER: I wasn't speaking of Shigalov or of his ideas, which bear the mark of genius, of course, but I meant all such discussions.

LIPUTIN: By discussing, one might reach a result. That is better than maintaining silence while posing as a dictator.

[*All approve this direct blow.*]

PETER: Writing and constructing systems is just nonsense. An aesthetic pastime. You are simply bored here, that's all.

LIPUTIN: We are merely provincial, to be sure, and therefore worthy of pity. But up to now you haven't brought out anything sensational either. Those tracts you gave us say that universal society will be improved only by lopping off a hundred million heads. That doesn't seem to me any easier to put into practice than Shigalov's ideas.

PETER: The fact is that by lopping off a hundred million heads you progress faster, obviously.

THE SEMINARIST: You also run the risk of getting your own head lopped off.

PETER: It's a disadvantage. And that's the risk you always run when you try to establish a new religion. But I can very well understand, sir, that you would hesitate. And I consider that you have the right to withdraw.

THE SEMINARIST: I didn't say that. And I am ready to bind myself definitively to an organization if it proves serious and efficient.

PETER: What, you would be willing to take an oath of allegiance to the group we are organizing?

THE SEMINARIST: That is to say.... Why not, if...

PETER: Listen, gentlemen, I can understand very well that you expect from me explanations and revelations about the workings of our organization. But I cannot give them to you unless I am sure of you unto death. So let me ask you a question. Are you in favour of endless discussions or in favour of millions of heads? Of course, this is merely an image. In other words, are you in favour of wallowing in the swamp or of crossing it at full speed?

LYAMSHIN [*gaily*]: At full speed, of course, at full speed! Why wallow?

PETER: Are you therefore in agreement as to the methods set forth in the tracts I gave you?

THE SEMINARIST: That is to say.... Why, of course.... But they still have to be specified!

PETER: If you are afraid, there is no point in specifying.

THE SEMINARIST: No one here is afraid and you know it. But you are treating us like pawns on a chessboard. Explain things to us clearly and we can consider them with you.

PETER: Are you ready to bind yourself to the organization by oath?

VIRGINSKY: Certainly, if you ask it of us decently.

PETER [*nodding towards* SHATOV]: Liputin, you haven't said anything.

LIPUTIN: I am ready to answer that question and any others. But I should first like to be sure that there is no stool pigeon here.

[*Tumult.* LYAMSHIN *rushes to the piano.*]

PETER [*apparently very much alarmed*]: What? What do you mean? You alarm me. Is it possible that there is a spy among us?

[*All talk at once.*]

LIPUTIN: We would be compromised!

PETER: I'd be more compromised than you. Hence, you must all answer a question which will decide whether we are to separate or go on. If one of you learned that a murder was being prepared for the good of the cause, would he go and warn the police? [*To* THE SEMINARIST] Allow me to ask you first.

THE SEMINARIST: Why me first?

PETER: I don't know you so well.

THE SEMINARIST: Such a question is an insult.

PETER: Be more precise.

THE SEMINARIST [*furious*]: I would not denounce the group, of course not.

PETER: And you, Virginsky?

VIRGINSKY: No, a hundred times no!

LIPUTIN: But why is Shatov getting up?

[SHATOV *has in fact stood up. Pale with wrath, he stares at* PETER VERKHOVENSKY *and then strides towards the door.*]

PETER: Your attitude may harm you greatly, Shatov.

SHATOV: At least it may be useful to the spy and scoundrel that you are. So be satisfied. I shall not stoop to answering your vicious question.

[*He goes out. Tumult. Everyone has got up except* STAVROGIN. KIRILOV *goes slowly back into his room.* PETER VERKHOVENSKY *drinks another glass of cognac.*]

LIPUTIN: Well! The test has done some good. Now we know. [STAVROGIN *gets up.*]

LYAMSHIN: Stavrogin didn't answer either.

VIRGINSKY: Stavrogin, can you answer the question?

STAVROGIN: I don't see the need of it.

VIRGINSKY: But we all compromised ourselves and you didn't!

STAVROGIN: Well, then, you will be compromised and I won't be.

[*Tumult.*]

THE SEMINARIST: But Verkhovensky didn't answer the question either.

STAVROGIN: To be sure. [*He goes out.*]

[PETER VERKHOVENSKY *rushes after him and then returns suddenly.*]

PETER: Listen. Stavrogin is the delegate. You must all obey him, and also me, his second unto death. Unto death, you understand. And remember that Shatov has just clearly taken his stand as a traitor and that traitors must be punished. Take an oath. . . . Come now, take an oath . . .

THE SEMINARIST: To what?

PETER: Are you men or aren't you? And will you hesitate before an oath of honour?

VIRGINSKY [*somewhat bewildered*]: But what must we swear?

PETER: To punish traitors. Quickly, take an oath. Hurry, now. I must catch up with Stavrogin. Take an oath . . .

[*They all raise their hands very slowly.* PETER VERKHOVENSKY *rushes outside.*]

BLACKOUT

SCENE THIRTEEN

First in the street and then at Varvara Stavrogin's. STAVROGIN *and* PETER VERKHOVENSKY.

PETER [*running after* STAVROGIN]: Why did you leave?

STAVROGIN: I had had enough. And your comedy with Shatov nauseated me. But I'll not let you get away with it.

PETER: He put the finger on himself.

STAVROGIN [*stopping*]: You are a liar. I have already told you why you needed Shatov's blood. He is to serve you to cement your group together. You've just succeeded very cleverly in getting him to leave. You knew that he would refuse to say 'I shall not denounce the group'. ||And that he would consider it cowardly to answer you.||

PETER: All right, all right! But you shouldn't have left. I need you.

STAVROGIN: I suspect as much, since you want to push me into having my wife slaughtered. But why? How can I be useful to you?

PETER: How? Why, in every way. . . . Besides, you spoke the truth. Be on my side and I shall get rid of your wife for you. [PETER VERKHOVENSKY *grasps* STAVROGIN *by the arm.* STAVROGIN *tears himself away, seizes him by the hair, and flings him to the ground.*] Oh, you are strong! Stavrogin, do what I ask of you and tomorrow I shall bring you Lisa Drozdov. Will you? Answer! Listen, I'll let you keep Shatov too if you ask me to.

STAVROGIN: So it's true that you have made up your mind to kill him?

PETER [*getting up*]: How can that matter to you? Wasn't he mean to you?

STAVROGIN: Shatov is good. *You* are mean.

PETER: I am. But *I* didn't slap you.

STAVROGIN: If you raised a hand against me, I'd kill you on the spot. You know very well that I can kill.

PETER: I know it. But you won't kill me because you despise me.

STAVROGIN: You are perspicacious. [*He walks away.*]

PETER: Listen! Listen . . .

[PETER *gives a signal.* FEDKA *appears, and together they follow* STAVROGIN. *The curtain representing the street rises to show Varvara Stavrogin's drawing-room.* DASHA *is on the stage. Hearing* PETER VERKHOVENSKY'*s voice, she goes out on the right.* STAVROGIN *and* PETER VERKHOVENSKY *enter.*]

PETER: Listen . . .

STAVROGIN: You are obstinate. . . . Tell me once and for all what you expect of me and leave.

PETER: Yes, yes. All right. [*He looks at the door on the side.*] Just a minute. [*He goes towards the door and opens it carefully.*]

STAVROGIN: My mother never listens at doors.

PETER: I'm sure she doesn't. You nobles are far above that.

I, on the contrary, listen at doors. Besides, I thought I heard a sound. But that's not the question. You want to know what I expect of you? [STAVROGIN *is silent.*] Well, this is it.... Together we'll rouse Russia and lift her from the mire.

STAVROGIN: She is heavy.

PETER: Ten more groups like this one and we'll be powerful.

STAVROGIN: Ten groups of idiots like these!

||PETER: It's idiots who make history. For instance, just look at the governor's wife, Julia Mikhailovna. She is with us. How incredibly stupid!

STAVROGIN: You are not going to tell me that she is plotting?

PETER: No. But her idea is that Russian youth must be kept from heading towards the abyss – and by that she means towards revolution. Her system is simple. The thing to do is to praise revolution, to be on the side of youth, and to show them that it is quite possible to be a revolutionary and the governor's wife. Then youth will realize that this is the best régime, since you can insult it without danger and even be rewarded for planning its destruction.

STAVROGIN: You must be exaggerating. It isn't possible to be all that stupid.||

PETER: Oh, they are not so stupid; they're just idealists. Fortunately, *I* am not idealist. But I am not intelligent either. What?

STAVROGIN: I didn't say anything.

PETER: Too bad. I hoped you would say: 'Why yes, you are intelligent.'

STAVROGIN: I never thought of saying anything of the sort.

PETER [*with hatred in his voice*]: You are right; I am stupid.

That's why I need you. My organization does not have a head.

STAVROGIN: You have Shigalov. [*He yawns.*]

PETER [*with the same hatred in his voice*]: Don't make fun of him. Absolute levelling is an excellent idea – not at all ridiculous. It's one of the elements of my plan. We shall have to organize it carefully. People will be forced to spy on one another and to denounce one another. In that way there'll be no more selfishness! From time to time a few convulsions, carefully controlled, just enough to overcome boredom. ||We leaders will take care of that. For there will be leaders, since there must be slaves.|| Hence total obedience, absolute depersonalization, and every thirty years we shall authorize convulsions, and then everyone will fall on one another and devour one another.

STAVROGIN [*looking at him*]: I have wondered for a long time what you resembled. But I made the mistake of looking for my comparison in the animal kingdom. It has just come to me.

PETER [*his mind on other things*]: Yes, yes.

STAVROGIN: You resemble a Jesuit.

PETER: All right, all right. But the Jesuits have the idea. They discovered the formula. The plot, the lie, and a single aim! Impossible to live otherwise in the world. Besides, we shall have to have the Pope on our side.

STAVROGIN: The Pope?

PETER: Yes, but it's very complicated. First the Pope would have to come to an agreement with the International. It's too soon for that. That will come inevitably later on, because it's the same spirit. Then there will be the Pope at the summit, we around him, and beneath us the masses governed by Shigalov's system. But that's an idea for the future. Meanwhile, work must be divided. So in the West there will be the Pope, and among us . . . among us . . . there will be you.

STAVROGIN: Decidedly you are drunk. Get out.

PETER: Stavrogin, you are handsome. Are you aware that you are handsome, and strong, and intelligent? No, you don't know it, for you are also unsophisticated. *I* do know it, and that's why you are my idol. I am a nihilist, and nihilists need idols. ||You are the man we need. You never insult anyone and yet everyone hates you. You treat people as your equals and yet they are afraid of you. But you are afraid of nothing; you can sacrifice your own life as easily as anyone else's. That is excellent. || Yes, you are the man I need, and I can't think of any other. You are the leader, you are the sun. [*He suddenly seizes* STAVROGIN'*s hand and kisses it.* STAVROGIN *repulses him.*] Don't despise me. Shigalov has found the system, but I alone have discovered the way of putting it into practice. I need you. Without you I am nothing. With you I shall destroy the old Russia and build the new.

STAVROGIN: What Russia? The Russia of spies?

PETER: When we hold power in our hands, we shall be able perhaps to make people more virtuous, if you really insist. But for the moment, to be sure, we need one or two thoroughly immoral generations; we need an exceptional, revolting corruption that will transform man into a filthy, cowardly, and selfish insect. That's what we need. And, on the side, we'll give them a touch of fresh blood so that they'll get a taste for it.

STAVROGIN: I always knew you weren't a socialist. You're a scoundrel.

PETER: All right, all right. A scoundrel. But let me explain my plan. We begin the general upheaval. Fires, crimes, incessant strikes, everything a mockery. You see what I mean? Oh, it will be wonderful! A heavy fog will descend over Russia. The earth will bewail its former gods. And then ... [*He pauses.*]

STAVROGIN: And then ...

PETER: We shall bring forth the new Tsar.

[STAVROGIN *looks at him and moves slowly away from him.*]

STAVROGIN: I see. An impostor.

PETER: Yes. We'll say that he is hiding but that he is about to appear. He exists, but no one has seen him. Just imagine the force of that idea – 'He is in hiding'! He can be shown perhaps to one out of a hundred thousand. And the rumour will spread over the whole country. 'He has been seen.' Will you accept?

STAVROGIN: Accept what?

PETER: Why, being the new Tsar.

STAVROGIN: Ah! So that's your plan!

PETER: Yes. Just listen. With you it will be possible to build up a legend. You will have only to appear and you will be triumphant. At first, 'he is hiding, he is hiding,' and we shall pronounce in your name two or three judgments of Solomon. If one request out of ten thousand is satisfied, all will turn to you. In every village each peasant will know that somewhere there is a box in which he can put his request. And throughout the country the rumour will spread! 'A new law has been passed, a just law.' The seas will rise up and the old wooden hulk will sink. And then we can think of building in steel. Well? [STAVROGIN *laughs in scorn.*] Oh, Stavrogin, don't leave me alone. Without you I am like Columbus without America. Can you imagine Columbus without America? I, in turn, can help you. I'll fix everything for you. Tomorrow I'll bring you Lisa. You want her; you want Lisa dreadfully, I know. Just one word and I'll fix everything.

STAVROGIN [*turning towards the window*]: And afterwards, of course, you will have a hold on me . . .

PETER: What does that matter? *You* will have a hold on Lisa. She is young and pure . . .

STAVROGIN [*with an odd expression, as if fascinated*]: She is pure . . .

[PETER VERKHOVENSKY *whistles piercingly.*] What are you doing? [FEDKA *appears.*]

PETER: Here is a friend who can help us. Just say yes, Stavrogin – a simple yes – and Lisa is yours, and the world is ours.

[STAVROGIN *turns towards* FEDKA, *who is smiling calmly. From another room* DASHA *screams, bursts in, and throws herself on* STAVROGIN.]

DASHA: Oh, Nicholas, I beg you, don't stay with these men. Go and see Tihon – yes, Tihon, as I have already told you. Go and see Tihon.

PETER: Tihon? Who is that?

FEDKA: A holy man. Don't say anything bad about him, you little sneak; I forbid you.

PETER: Why? Did he help you kill someone? Does he too belong to the Church of Blood?

FEDKA: No. *I* kill. But *he* forgives crime.

BLACKOUT

THE NARRATOR: Personally, I didn't know Tihon. I simply knew what was said of him in our town. The humble people attributed great holiness to him. But the authorities disapproved of his library, in which works of piety stood side by side with plays and perhaps even worse.

Offhand, I'd say there was no chance Stavrogin would pay him a visit.

SCENE FOURTEEN

Tihon's cell in the Convent of the Virgin. TIHON *and* STAVROGIN *are standing.*

STAVROGIN: Did my mother tell you I was mad?

TIHON: No. She didn't talk of you exactly as of a madman. But she told me of a slap you received and of a duel ... [*He sits down with a groan.*]

STAVROGIN: Are you ill?

TIHON: I have pains in my legs. And I don't sleep very well.

STAVROGIN: Do you want me to leave you?

TIHON: No. Sit down! [STAVROGIN *sits down with his hat in his hand, like a man observing ceremony. But he seems to have trouble breathing.*] You too look ill.

STAVROGIN [*with the same manner*]: I am. You see, I have hallucinations. I often see or feel near me a sort of creature who is mocking, wicked, rational, and who takes on different aspects. But it's always the same creature. He drives me wild. I shall have to consult a doctor.

TIHON: Yes. Do so.

STAVROGIN: No, it's useless. I know who it is. And you do too.

TIHON: You mean the Devil?

STAVROGIN: Yes. You believe in him, don't you? A man of your calling is obliged to believe in him.

TIHON: Well, I'd say that in your case it is more probably an ailment.

STAVROGIN: You are sceptical, I see. Do you at least believe in God?

TIHON: I believe in God.

STAVROGIN: It is written: 'If you believe and if you command the mountain to be removed, you shall be obeyed.' Can you move a mountain?

TIHON: Perhaps. With the help of God.

STAVROGIN: Why 'perhaps'? If you believe, you must say yes.

TIHON: My faith is imperfect.

STAVROGIN: Well, it's a pity. Do you know the answer that a certain bishop made? With the knife at his throat, a barbarian asked him if he believed in God. 'Very little, very little,' the bishop replied. That's not worthy, is it?

TIHON: His faith was imperfect.

STAVROGIN [*smiling*]: Yes, yes. But, in my opinion, faith must be perfect or there is no faith. That's why I'm an atheist.

TIHON: The complete atheist is more respectable than the man who is indifferent. He is on the last rung preceding perfect faith.

STAVROGIN: I know it. Do you remember the passage from the Apocalypse about the lukewarm?

TIHON: Yes. 'I know thy works, that thou art neither cold nor hot: I would thou wert cold or hot. So then because thou art lukewarm, and neither cold nor hot, I will spew thee out of my mouth. Because thou sayest ...'

STAVROGIN: That will do. [*A silence. Without looking at him*] You know, I like you very much.

TIHON [*in a whisper*]: I like you too. [*Rather long silence. Stroking* STAVROGIN's *elbow with his finger*] Don't be annoyed.

STAVROGIN [*giving a start*]: How did you know ... [*He*

resumes his normal tone of voice.] Indeed, yes, I was annoyed because I told you that I liked you.

TIHON [*firmly*]: Don't be annoyed, and tell me everything.

STAVROGIN: So you are sure that I came with an ulterior motive?

TIHON [*lowering his eyes*]: I read it on your face when you came in.

[STAVROGIN *is pale and his hands tremble. He takes several sheets of paper out of his pocket.*]

STAVROGIN: All right. I wrote a story about myself which I am going to publish. Whatever you may say to me about it won't change my decision in any way. However, I should like you to be the first to know this story, and I'm going to tell it to you. [TIHON *slowly nods his head.*] Stop up your ears. Promise not to listen to me and I shall speak. [TIHON *doesn't answer.*] From 1861 to 1863 I lived in Petersburg indulging in debaucheries that provided no pleasure. I was living with nihilist comrades who adored me because of my money. I was dreadfully bored. So much so that I might have hanged myself. ||The reason that I didn't hang myself then is that I was hoping for something, I didn't know just what.|| [TIHON *says nothing.*] I had three apartments.

TIHON: Three?

STAVROGIN: Yes. One in which I had set up Maria Lebyatkin, who later became my legitimate wife. And two others in which I used to receive my mistresses. One of them was rented to me by shopkeepers, who occupied the rest of the apartment and worked elsewhere. Hence I was alone there, rather often, with their twelve-year-old daughter named Matriocha. [*He stops.*]

TIHON: Do you want to go on or stop there?

STAVROGIN: I'll go on. She was a very gentle and calm child, pale blonde and freckled. One day I couldn't find my pocket knife. I mentioned it to the mother, who accused her daughter and beat her, in my presence, until she bled. That evening I found the pocket-knife in the folds of my blanket. I put it into my waistcoat pocket and, once outside, threw it away in the street so that no one would know about it. Three days later I went back to Matriocha's house. [*He stops.*]

TIHON: Did you tell her parents?

STAVROGIN: No. They weren't there. Matriocha was alone.

TIHON: Ah!

STAVROGIN: Yes. Alone. She was sitting in a corner on a little bench. She had her back turned. For some time I watched her from my room. Suddenly she began to sing softly, very softly. My heart began beating violently. I got up and slowly approached Matriocha. ||The windows were decorated with geraniums; the sun was hot.|| I sat down silently beside her on the floor. She was frightened and suddenly stood up. I took her hand and kissed it; she laughed like a child; I made her sit down again, but she again got up with a frightened look. I kissed her hand again. I drew her on to my lap. She withdrew a bit and smiled again. I was laughing too. Then she threw her arms around my neck and kissed me . . . [*He stops.* TIHON *looks at him.* STAVROGIN *stares back at him and then, showing a blank sheet*] At this point in my story I left a blank.

TIHON: Are you going to tell me what followed?

STAVROGIN [*laughing awkwardly, his face distorted*]: No, no. Later on. When you become worthy of it . . . [TIHON *stares at him.*] But nothing happened at all; what are you thinking? Nothing at all. . . . It would be better if you didn't look at me. [*In a whisper*] And don't try my patience.

[TIHON *lowers his eyes.*] When I returned two days later, Matriocha fled into the other room as soon as she saw me. But it was clear to me that she hadn't said anything to her mother. Yet I was afraid. During that whole time I was horribly afraid that she would talk. Finally, one day her mother told me, before leaving us alone, that the girl was in bed with a fever. I sat down in my room and, without stirring, watched the bed in the darkness of the other room. An hour later she moved. She came out of the darkness, emaciated in her nightgown, came to the door of my room, and there, tossing her head, shook her frail little fist at me. Then she fled. I heard her run along the inner balcony. I got up and saw her disappear into a nook where wood was kept. I knew what she was going to do. But I sat down again and forced myself to wait twenty minutes. ||Someone was singing in the courtyard; a fly was buzzing near me. I caught it, held it in my hand a moment, and then let it go.|| I recall that on a geranium near me a tiny red spider was walking slowly. When the twenty minutes were up, I forced myself to wait a quarter of an hour more. Then, as I left, I looked into the nook through a crack. Matriocha had hanged herself. I left and spent the evening playing cards, with the feeling that a weight had been lifted from me.

TIHON: A weight lifted from you?

STAVROGIN [*with a change in manner*]: Yes. But at the same time I knew that the feeling was based on a horrible cowardice and that never again, never again, could I feel noble in this life, or in another life, never . . .

TIHON: Is that why you acted so strangely here?

STAVROGIN: Yes. I should have liked to kill myself. But I didn't have the courage. So I ruined my life in the stupidest way possible. I led an ironic life. It occurred to me that it would be a good idea – quite stupid, really – to marry a crazy woman, a cripple, and so I did. I even accepted a duel and kept from shooting in the hope of being killed foolishly. Finally I accepted the heaviest responsibilities, without believing in them. But all that was in vain! And now I live between two dreams. In one of them there are happy islands surrounded by a sun-drenched sea where men wake up and go to bed innocent, and in the other I see an emaciated Matriocha tossing her head and shaking her little fist at me. . . . Her little fist . . . I should like to erase a deed from my life, and I cannot.

[*He hides his head in his hands. Then, after a silence, he straightens up.*]

TIHON: Are you really going to publish this story?

STAVROGIN: Yes. Yes!

TIHON: Your intention is noble. The spirit of penitence can go no further. It would be an admirable action to punish oneself this way if only . . .

STAVROGIN: If?

TIHON: If only it were a true penance.

STAVROGIN: What do you mean?

TIHON: You express directly in your narrative the need felt by a heart mortally wounded. This is why you wanted to be spat upon, to be slapped, and to be shamed. But at the same time there is pride and defiance in your confession. ||Sensuality and idleness have made you insensitive, incapable of loving, and you seem to be proud of that insensitivity. You are proud of what is shameful.|| That is despicable.

STAVROGIN: I thank you.

TIHON: Why?

STAVROGIN: Because, although you are annoyed with me,

you don't seem to feel any disgust and you talk to me as to an equal.

TIHON: I was disgusted. But you have so much pride that you didn't notice it. Yet your words 'You talk to me as an equal' are beautiful words. They show that your heart is great and your strength tremendous. But that great useless strength in you frightens me because it seeks to express itself only in foul deeds. You have negated everything, you no longer love anything, and a punishment pursues all those who break away from their native soil, from the truth belonging to their own people and their own time.

STAVROGIN: I don't fear that punishment, or any other.

TIHON: One must fear, on the contrary. Or else there is no punishment but only delight. Listen. If someone, someone you didn't know, whom you would never see again, read that confession and forgave you silently in his heart, would that bring you peace?

STAVROGIN: That would bring me peace. [*In a whisper*] If you forgave me, that would do me great good. [*He stares at him and then breaks out in violent passion.*] No! I want to win my own forgiveness! That is my principal and sole aim. Only then will the vision disappear! That is why I long for an exceptional suffering; that is why I seek it myself! Don't discourage me or I shall burst with rage!

TIHON [*rising*]: If you believe that you can forgive yourself, and that you will achieve your forgiveness in this world through suffering, if you seek solely to obtain that forgiveness – oh, then you have complete faith! God will forgive you ||your absence of faith, for you venerate the Holy Ghost without knowing it||.

STAVROGIN: There can be no forgiveness for me. It is

written in your books that there is no greater crime than to offend one of these little ones.

TIHON: If you forgive yourself, Christ will forgive you likewise.

STAVROGIN: No. No. Not He. There can be no forgiveness! Never again, never again . . .

[STAVROGIN *takes his hat and strides towards the door like a madman. But he turns back towards* TIHON *and resumes his ceremonious manner. He seems exhausted.*] I shall return. We shall talk of all this again. I assure you that I'm very happy to have met you. I appreciate your welcome and your understanding.

TIHON: Are you leaving already? I wanted to ask you a favour. . . . But I fear . . .

STAVROGIN: Please do. [*He negligently picks up a little crucifix from the table.*]

TIHON: Don't publish that story.

STAVROGIN: I warned you that nothing will stop me. I shall make it known to the whole world!

TIHON: I understand. But I propose to you an even greater sacrifice. Give up your intention and in this way you will overcome your pride, you will crush your demon, and you will achieve liberty. [*He clasps his hands.*]

STAVROGIN: You take all this too much to heart. If I listened to you, I'd just settle down, have children, become a member of a club, and come to the monastery on holy days.

TIHON: No. I am suggesting a different penance. In this monastery there is an ascetic, an old man of such Christian wisdom that neither I nor even you can imagine it. Go to him, submit to his authority for five or seven years, and you will obtain, I promise you, everything for which you thirst.

STAVROGIN [*in a bantering tone of voice*]: Enter the monastery? Why not? After all, I am convinced that I could live like a monk, although I am gifted with a bestial sensuality. [TIHON *cries out, with his hands stretched in front of him.*] What's the matter?

TIHON: I see, I see clearly that you have never been closer to committing another crime even more heinous than the one you have just related.

STAVROGIN: Calm yourself. I can promise you not to publish this story immediately.

TIHON: No. No. There will come a day, an hour, before that great sacrifice, when you will look for a way out in a new crime, and you will commit it only to avoid publication of these pages! [STAVROGIN *stares at him fixedly, breaks the crucifix, and drops the pieces on the table.*]

CURTAIN

THIRD PART

SCENE FIFTEEN

At Varvara Stavrogin's. STAVROGIN *comes in, his face distorted, hesitates, wheels around, and then disappears through the door upstage.* GRIGORIEV *and* STEPAN TROFIMOVICH *come in, greatly excited.*

STEPAN: But, after all, what does she want of me?
GRIGORIEV: I don't know. She asked you to come at once.
STEPAN: It must be the house search. She heard of it. She will never forgive me.
GRIGORIEV: But who came to search you?
STEPAN: I don't know, *une espèce d'Allemand,* who directed everything. I was excited. He talked. No, I was the one who talked. I told him my whole life – from the political point of view, I mean. I was excited but dignified, I assure you. Yet . . . I fear I may have wept.
GRIGORIEV: But you should have demanded his search warrant. You should have shown a little arrogance.
STEPAN: Listen, Anton, don't criticize me. When you are unhappy, there is nothing more unbearable than having friends tell you that you have made a mistake. In any case, I have taken my precautions. I have had warm clothing packed.
GRIGORIEV: For what reason?
STEPAN: Well, if they come to get me. . . . That's the way it is now: they come, they seize you, and then Siberia or worse. Consequently I sewed thirty-five roubles into the lining of my waistcoat.

GRIGORIEV: But there's no question of your being arrested.

STEPAN: They must have received a telegram from St Petersburg.

GRIGORIEV: About you? But you haven't done anything.

STEPAN: Yes, yes, I'll be arrested. And off to prison, or else they forget you in a dungeon. [*He bursts into sobs.*]

GRIGORIEV: Come, come, calm yourself. You haven't anything on your conscience. Why are you afraid?

STEPAN: Afraid? Oh, I'm not afraid! I mean, I'm not afraid of Siberia. There's something else I fear. I fear shame.

GRIGORIEV: Shame? What shame?

STEPAN: The whip!

GRIGORIEV: What do you mean, the whip? You frighten me, my friend.

STEPAN: Yes, they flog you too.

GRIGORIEV: But why should they flog you? You haven't done anything.

STEPAN: That's just it. They'll see that I haven't done anything and they'll flog me.

GRIGORIEV: You should take a rest after you have seen Varvara Stavrogin.

STEPAN: What will she think? How will she react when she learns of my shame? Here she is. [*He makes the sign of the cross.*]

GRIGORIEV: You make the sign of the cross?

STEPAN: Oh, I've never believed in that. But, after all, it's better not to take any chances.

[VARVARA STAVROGIN *comes in. They rise.*]

VARVARA [*to* GRIGORIEV]: Thank you, Anton. Would you be so kind as to leave us alone? . . . [*To* STEPAN TROFIMOVICH] Sit down. [GRIGORIEV *leaves. She goes to the desk and writes a note rapidly. Meanwhile,* STEPAN TROFIMOVICH *squirms on his chair. Then she turns around towards him.*] Stepan Trofimovich, we have questions to settle before separating definitively. I shall be blunt. [*He cringes on his chair.*] Don't say a word. Let me do the talking. I consider myself committed to continuing your allowance of twelve hundred roubles. I am adding eight hundred roubles for exceptional expenses. Is that enough for you? It seems to me that it is not negligible. So you will take this money and go to live, as you will, in Petersburg, in Moscow, abroad, but not in my house. Do you understand?

STEPAN: Not long ago you made another arbitrary demand, just as urgent and just as categorical. I submitted to it. I disguised myself as a fiancé and danced the minuet for love of you . . .

VARVARA: You didn't dance. You came to my house wearing a new necktie, pomaded and perfumed. You had an urgent desire to get married; it could be seen on your face, and, take my word for it, it was not pretty to see. Especially with an innocent young girl, almost a child . . .

STEPAN: Please let's not talk about it any more. I shall go to a home for the aged.

VARVARA: People don't go to a home for the aged when they have an income of two thousand roubles. ||You say that because your son, who, by the way is more intelligent than you say he is, joked one day about a home. But there are all sorts of homes and there are even some that take in generals. So you could have a game of whist there . . .||

STEPAN: *Passons.* Let's not mention it.

VARVARA: *Passons?* So you are becoming rude now? In that case, let's end our conversation right here. You are forewarned: henceforth we shall live apart.

STEPAN: And that's all? That's all that remains of our twenty years together? Is that our final farewell?

VARVARA: Yes, what about those twenty years! Twenty years of vanity and posturing! Even the letters you sent me were written for posterity. You are not a friend; you are a stylist!

STEPAN: You talk like my son. I see that he has influenced you.

VARVARA: So, you don't think I'm big enough to think for myself? What have you done for me during these twenty years? You even refused me the books that I ordered for you. You wouldn't give them to me until you had read them yourself, and since you never read them I had to wait for them twenty years. The truth is that you were jealous of my intellectual development.

STEPAN [*in despair*]: But is it possible to break off everything for so little reason!

VARVARA: When I came back from abroad and wanted to tell you my impressions of the Sistine Madonna, you didn't even listen to me; you simply smiled with an air of superiority.

STEPAN: I smiled, yes, but I didn't feel superior.

VARVARA: There was no reason to, in any case! No one is interested in that Sistine Madonna except a few old simpletons like you. That's obvious.

STEPAN: What is obvious, after all these cruel words, is that I must leave. Mark my words: I shall take up my beggar's staff and bag; I shall leave all your gifts and I'll start out on foot to end my life as a tutor in the home of some shopkeeper or die of hunger in a ditch. Farewell.

[VARVARA STAVROGIN *rises, exploding*.]

VARVARA: I was sure of it. I have known for years that you were simply waiting for the chance to dishonour me. You are capable of dying just so that my house will be slandered.

STEPAN: You have always despised me. But I shall end my life like a knight faithful to his lady. From this minute forward, I shall accept nothing more from you and shall honour you in a disinterested way.

VARVARA: *That* will be new.

STEPAN: I know, you have never had any regard for me. Yes. I was your parasite and I was occasionally weak. But to live as a parasite never was the ruling principle of my conduct. It just happened, I don't know how. I always thought there was something between us over and above eating and drinking, and I never was vulgar. Well, now I'll take to the road to right my wrongs! It is very late, the autumn is well along, the countryside is thick in fog, the frost of old age covers my way, and in the howling of the wind I can hear the call of the grave. *En route, cependant!* Oh, I say farewell to you, my dreams! *Vingt ans!* [*His face is covered with tears.*] *Allons!*

VARVARA [*she is deeply moved, but stamps her foot*]: ||This is just one more bit of childishness. You will never be capable of carrying out your selfish threats. You won't go anywhere, you won't find any shopkeepers, and you will remain on my neck, continuing to draw your allowance and to receive your dreadful friends every Tuesday.|| Farewell, Stepan Trofimovich!

STEPAN: *Alea jacta est.* [*He rushes out*].

VARVARA: Stepan!

[*But he has disappeared. She walks in circles, tearing her muff to pieces, then flings herself on the sofa in tears. Outside, vague noises.*]

GRIGORIEV [*coming in*]: Where was Stepan Trofimovich going? And there is an uprising in town!

VARVARA: An uprising?

GRIGORIEV: Yes. The workers from Spigulin's factory are holding a demonstration in front of the governor's house. The governor himself is reported to have gone mad.

VARVARA: Good Lord, Stepan may get caught in the uprising!

[*There enter, ushered in by* ALEXEY YEGOROVICH: PRASCOVYA DROZDOV, LISA, MAURICE NICOLAEVICH *and* DASHA.]

PRASCOVYA: Oh! Good heavens! It's the revolution! And my poor legs that can't drag me any further.

[*There enter* VIRGINSKY, LIPUTIN, *and* PETER VERKHOVENSKY.]

PETER: Things are stirring, things are stirring. That idiot of a governor had an attack of brain fever.

VARVARA: Have you seen your father?

PETER: No, but he's not running any risk. He might be flogged, but that will do him good.

[STAVROGIN *appears. His necktie is twisted out of place. He looks a bit mad, for the first time.*]

VARVARA: Nicholas, what's the matter with you?

STAVROGIN: Nothing. Nothing. It seemed to me that someone was calling me. No. . . . No. . . . Who would call me?

[LISA *takes a step forward.*]

LISA: Nicholas Stavrogin, a certain Lebyatkin, who calls himself your wife's brother, is sending me improper letters claiming to have revelations to make about you. If he is really your relative, keep him from bothering me.

[VARVARA *rushes towards* LISA.]

STAVROGIN [*with strange simplicity*]: I have in fact the misfortune of being related to that man. It is four years now since I married his sister, née Lebyatkin, in Petersburg.

[VARVARA *lifts up her right arm as if to shield her face and falls in a faint. All rush towards her except* LISA *and* STAVROGIN.]

STAVROGIN [*in the same tone of voice*]: Now is the time to follow me, Lisa. We shall go to my country house at Skvoreshniki.

[LISA *walks towards him like an automaton.* MAURICE NICOLAEVICH, *who was paying attention to* VARVARA PETROVNA, *rises and rushes towards her.*]

MAURICE: Lisa!

[*A gesture on her part stops him.*]

LISA: Have pity on me. [*She follows* STAVROGIN.]

BLACKOUT

THE NARRATOR [*in front of a curtain lighted by the burning city*]: The fire that had been smouldering for so long finally burst forth. It first burst out in reality the night that Lisa followed Stavrogin. The fire destroyed the suburb separating Stavrogin's country house from the town. In that suburb stood the house lived in by Lebyatkin and his sister, Maria. But the fire burst forth likewise in people's souls. After Lisa's flight misfortune followed misfortune.

SCENE SIXTEEN

The drawing-room of the country house at Skvoreshniki. Six a.m. LISA, *wearing the same dress, which is now rumpled and badly hooked up, is standing by the french window watching the fires of the city. She shudders.* STAVROGIN *comes in from the outside.*

STAVROGIN: Alexey has gone on horseback to get news. In a few minutes we shall know all. It is said that a part of the suburb has already burned down. The fire broke out between eleven and midnight.

[LISA *turns around suddenly and goes over and sits down in an armchair.*]

LISA: Listen to me, Nicholas. We haven't much longer to be together and I want to say all I have to say.

STAVROGIN: What do you mean, Lisa? Why haven't we much longer to be together?

LISA: Because I am dead.

STAVROGIN: Dead? Why, Lisa? You must live.

LISA: You have forgotten that as we arrived here yesterday I told you that you had brought a dead woman. I have lived since then. I have had my hour of life on earth, and that is enough. I don't want to be like Christofor Ivanovich. You remember?

STAVROGIN: Yes.

LISA: He bored you dreadfully, didn't he, at Lausanne? He always used to say: 'I have come just for a minute' and then he would stay all day. I don't want to be like him.

STAVROGIN: Don't talk like that. You are hurting yourself and hurting me too. I swear to you that I love you more at this moment than I did yesterday when we arrived here.

LISA: What an odd declaration!

STAVROGIN: We shan't separate again. We shall leave together.

LISA: Leave? Why? To be reborn together, as you said. No, all that is too sublime for me. If I were to leave with you, it would be for Moscow, to have a home and live among friends. That is my ideal, a very middle-class ideal. But, as you are married, all this is pointless.

STAVROGIN: But, Lisa, have you forgotten that you gave yourself to me?

LISA: I haven't forgotten it. I want to leave you now.

STAVROGIN: You are taking revenge on me for your whim of yesterday.

LISA: That is a thoroughly vulgar thought.

STAVROGIN: Then why did you do it?

LISA: What do you care? You are guilty of nothing; you don't have to answer to anyone.

STAVROGIN: Don't despise me like that. I fear nothing except losing the hope you gave me. I was lost, like a drowning man, and I thought that your love would save me. Do you have any idea what that new hope cost me? I paid for it with life itself.

LISA: Your life or someone else's?

STAVROGIN [*thoroughly upset*]: What do you mean? Tell me at once what you mean!

LISA: I simply asked you if you had paid for that hope with your life or mine. Why do you stare at me so? What did you think? You look as if you were afraid, as if you had been afraid for some time.... You are so pale now...

STAVROGIN: If you know something, *I* know nothing, I swear. That's not what I meant.

LISA [*terrified*]: I don't understand you.

STAVROGIN [*sitting down and hiding his face in his hands*]: A bad dream.... A nightmare.... We were talking of two different things.

LISA: I don't know what you were talking about... [*She stares at him.*] Nicholas... [*He raises his head.*] Is it possible that you didn't guess yesterday that I would leave you today? Did you know it – yes or no? Don't lie: did you know it?

STAVROGIN: I knew it.

LISA: You knew it and yet you took me.

STAVROGIN: Yes, condemn me. You have the right to do so. I knew also that I didn't love you and yet I took you. I have never felt love for anyone. I desire, that's all. And I took advantage of you. But I have always hoped that some day I could love, and I have always hoped that it would be you. The fact that you were willing to follow me gave strength to that hope. I shall love, yes, I shall love you . . .

LISA: You will love me! And I imagined. . . . Ah! I followed you through pride, in order to rival you in generosity; I followed you to ruin myself with you and to share your misfortune. [*She weeps.*] But, despite everything, I imagined that you loved me madly. And you. . . . You hope to love me some day. What a little fool I was! Don't make fun of these tears. I love being sentimental about myself. But that is enough! I am not capable of anything and you are not capable of anything either. Let us console ourselves by sticking out our tongues at each other. Like that our pride at least will not suffer.

STAVROGIN: Don't weep. I can't endure it.

LISA: I am calm. I gave my life for an hour with you. Now I am calm. As for you, you will forget. You will have other hours and other moments.

STAVROGIN: Never, never! No one but you . . .

LISA [*looking at him with a wild hope*]: Ah! You . . .

STAVROGIN: Yes, yes. I shall love you. Now I am sure of it. Some day my heart will relax at last, I shall bow my head and forget myself in your arms. You alone can cure me . . .

LISA [*who has recovered possession of herself, with a dull tone of despair*]: Cure you! I don't want to. I don't want to be a Sister of Charity for you. Ask Dasha instead; she will follow you everywhere like a dog. And don't worry about me. I knew in advance what was in store for me. I always knew that if I followed you, you would lead me to a spot inhabited by a monstrous spider as big as a man, that we would spend our life watching the spider and trembling with fear, and that our love would go no farther . . .

[ALEXEY YEGOROVICH *comes in.*]

ALEXEY: Sir, sir, they have found . . . [*He stops as he sees* LISA.] I . . . Sir, Peter Verkhovensky wishes to see you.

STAVROGIN: Lisa, wait in this room. [*She goes towards it.* ALEXEY YEGOROVICH *goes out.*] Lisa . . . [*She stops.*] If you hear anything, you might as well know now that *I* am the guilty one.

[*She looks at him in fright and slowly backs into the study.* PETER VERKHOVENSKY *comes in.*]

PETER: Let me tell you first of all that none of us is guilty. It was a mere coincidence. Legally, you are not involved . . .

STAVROGIN: They were burned? Assassinated?

PETER: Assassinated. Unfortunately, the house only half burned and the bodies were found. Lebyatkin's throat was slit. His sister had been slashed over and over again with a knife. But it was a prowler, most certainly. I have heard that, the night before, Lebyatkin was drunk and showed everybody the fifteen hundred roubles I had given him.

STAVROGIN: You had given him fifteen hundred roubles?

PETER: Yes. Quite deliberately. And from you.

STAVROGIN: From me?

PETER: Yes. I was afraid he would denounce us and I gave him the money so that he could get to St Petersburg . . . [STAVROGIN *takes a few steps with an absent-minded stare.*] But listen at least to the way things turned out . . . [*He grasps* STAVROGIN *by the lapel of his Prince Albert.* STAVROGIN *gives him a violent blow.*] Oh, you might have broken my arm! Of course, he boasted of having that money. Fedka saw it, that's all. I'm sure now that it was Fedka. He must not have understood your true intentions...

STAVROGIN [*oddly absent-minded*]: Was it Fedka who lighted the fire?

PETER: No. No. You know that such fires were planned in our group action. It's a very Russian way of starting a revolution.... But it came too soon! I was disobeyed, that's all, and I'll have to take steps. But don't forget that this misfortune has its advantages. For instance, you are a widower and you can marry Lisa tomorrow. Where is she? I want to give her the good news. [STAVROGIN *laughs suddenly, but with a sort of wild laugh.*] You are laughing?

STAVROGIN: Yes. I am laughing at one who apes me, I am laughing at you. Good news, indeed! But don't you think that those corpses will upset her somewhat?

PETER: Not at all! Why? Besides, legally.... And she's a young lady who isn't daunted by anything. You'll be amazed to see the way she steps over those corpses. Once she's married, she'll forget.

STAVROGIN: There will be no marriage. Lisa will remain alone.

PETER: No? As soon as I saw you together, I realized that it hadn't worked. Ah! A complete flop? ||I'll bet you spent the whole night seated on different chairs, wasting precious time discussing very serious things.|| Besides, I was sure that it would all end in nonsense.... Good. I shall easily marry her off to Maurice Nicolaevich, who must be waiting for her outside now in the rain. As for the others – the ones who were killed – it's better not to tell her anything about that. She'll find out soon enough. [LISA *comes in.*]

LISA: What shall I find out soon enough? Who has killed

someone? What did you say about Maurice Nicolaevich?

PETER: Well, young lady, so we listen at doors!

LISA: What did you say about Maurice Nicolaevich? Has he been killed?

STAVROGIN: No, Lisa. It was only my wife and her brother who were killed.

PETER [*in a hurry*]: A strange, a monstrous coincidence! Someone took advantage of the fire to kill and rob them. It must have been Fedka.

LISA: Nicholas! Is he telling the truth?

STAVROGIN: No. He is not telling the truth.

[LISA *moans.*]

PETER: But don't you see that this man has lost his reason! Besides he spent the night with you. Hence –

LISA: Nicholas, talk to me as if you stood before God at this moment. Are you guilty or not? I will trust your word as I would God's word. And I shall follow you, like a dog, to the end of the world.

STAVROGIN [*slowly*]: I did not kill and I was against that murder, but I knew they would be assassinated and I did not keep the murderers from doing it. Now, leave me.

LISA [*looking at him with horror*]: No! No! No! [*She rushes off, shouting.*]

PETER: So I have wasted my time with you!

STAVROGIN [*in a dull voice*]: Me. Oh! Me ... [*He laughs madly all of a sudden; then, getting up, shouts in a thunderous voice*] I loathe and detest everything that exists in Russia, the people, the Tsar, and you and Lisa. I hate everything that lives on earth, and myself first of all. So let destruction reign and crush them all, and with them all those who ape Stavrogin, and Stavrogin himself. . .

BLACKOUT

||SCENE SEVENTEEN*

In the street. LISA *is running.* PETER VERKHOVENSKY *is running after her.*

PETER: Wait, Lisa, wait. I'll take you home. I have a fiacre.

LISA [*bewildered*]: Yes, yes, you are good. Where are they? Where is the blood?

PETER: Stop! What can you do? It's raining, you see. Come. Maurice Nicolaevich is here.

LISA: Maurice! Where is he? Oh, my God, he's waiting for me! He knows!

PETER: What does that matter? Surely he doesn't have any prejudices!

LISA: Wonderful, wonderful! Ah, he mustn't see me. Let's flee in the woods, in the fields . . .

[PETER *leaves and* LISA *continues running.* MAURICE *appears and pursues her. She falls. He bends over her, weeping, takes off his coat, and covers her with it. She kisses his hand, weeping.*]

MAURICE: Lisa! I am nothing compared to you, but don't reject me!

LISA: Maurice, don't abandon me! I'm afraid of death. I don't want to die.

MAURICE: You are soaked! Good Lord! And it's still raining!

LISA: It doesn't matter. Come, lead me. I want to see the blood. They killed his wife, I've heard. And he says he was the one who killed her. But it's not true, is it? Oh, I must see with my own eyes those who were killed

*This scene was cut in production.

because of me.... Hurry! Hurry! Oh, Maurice, don't forgive me. I was wicked. Why should anyone forgive me? Why are you weeping? Strike me and kill me, right here!

MAURICE: No one has the right to judge you, and I least of all. May God forgive you!

[*Little by little the curtain is lighted by the flames of the fire, and the sound of the crowd can be heard.* STEPAN TROFIMOVICH *appears in travelling costume with a travelling bag in his left hand, a staff and an umbrella in his right hand.*]

STEPAN [*in delirium*]: Oh, you! *Chère, chère,* is it possible? In this fog.... You can see the fire!... You are unhappy, aren't you? I can see it. We are all unhappy, but we must forgive them all. To shake off the world and become free, *il faut pardonner, pardonner, pardonner* ...

LISA: Oh! Get up! Why are you kneeling?

STEPAN: At the moment of saying farewell to the world, I want to say farewell to you – and so to my whole past. [*He weeps.*] I am kneeling down before everything that was beautiful in my life. I dreamed of scaling the heights to heaven, and here I am in the mud, a crushed old man.... See their crime in all its red horror. They couldn't do otherwise. I am fleeing their delirium, their nightmare, and I am going in search of Russia. But you are both soaked. Here, take my umbrella. [MAURICE *automatically takes the umbrella.*] I'll find a cart of some kind. But, dear Lisa, what did you just say? Has someone been killed? [LISA *starts to swoon.*] Oh, my God, she is fainting!

LISA: Quick, quick, Maurice. Give this child back his umbrella! At once! [*She turns back towards* STEPAN TROFIMOVICH.] I want to make the sign of the cross over you, poor man. You, too, pray for poor Lisa!

[STEPAN TROFIMOVICH *goes off, and they walk towards the*

flames. The noise increases. The flames are becoming brighter. The crowd is now shouting.]

VOICES: It's Stavrogin's wench. It's not enough for them to kill people. They also want to see the bodies.

[*A man strikes* LISA. MAURICE NICOLAEVICH *throws himself on him. They fight.* LISA *picks herself up. Two other men strike her, one of them with a stick. She falls. Everything becomes calm.* MAURICE NICOLAEVICH *takes her in his arms and drags her towards the light.*]

MAURICE: Lisa, Lisa, don't forsake me. [LISA *falls back dead.*] Lisa, dear Lisa, now it's my turn to join you!

BLACKOUT||

THE NARRATOR: While they were looking everywhere for Stepan Trofimovich, who was wandering on the road like a deposed king, events were precipitated. Shatov's wife returned after three years' absence. But what Shatov took for a new beginning was in reality to be an end.

SCENE EIGHTEEN

Shatov's room. MARIA SHATOV *is standing with a travelling bag in her hand.*

MARIA: I'll not stay long, just long enough to find work. But if I am in your way, I beg you to tell me at once quite honestly. I'll sell something and go to the hotel. [*She sits down on the bed.*]

SHATOV: Maria, you mustn't talk of a hotel. You are at home here.

MARIA: No, I am not at home here. We separated three years ago. Don't get it into your head that I am repenting and coming back to begin over again.

SHATOV: No, no, that would be pointless. But it doesn't matter anyway. You are the only person who ever told me she loved me. That's enough. You are doing what you want, and now you are here.

MARIA: Yes, you are good. I have come back under your roof because I have always considered you a good man – so far above all those scoundrels . . .

SHATOV: Listen, Maria, you look exhausted. Please don't get annoyed. . . . If you'd only take a little tea, for instance. Tea always does one good. If you would only . . .

MARIA: Yes, I would. You are still just as much a child. Give me some tea if you have any. It's so cold here.

SHATOV: Yes, yes, you shall have tea.

MARIA: You don't have any here?

HATOV: There will be some. There will be some. [*He steps out and knocks at Kirilov's door.*] Can you lend me some tea?

KIRILOV: Come in and drink it!

SHATOV: No. My wife has come back. . .

KIRILOV: Your wife!

SHATOV [*sputtering and half weeping*]: Kirilov, Kirilov, we suffered together in America.

KIRILOV: Yes, yes, wait. [*He disappears and reappears with a tea tray.*] Here it is. Take it. And a rouble too – take it.

SHATOV: I'll give it back to you tomorrow! Ah, Kirilov!

KIRILOV: No, no, I am glad she has come back and that you still love her. I am glad that you turned to me. If you need anything, just call me at any time whatever. I shall be thinking of you and her.

SHATOV: Oh, what a man you would be if you could only get rid of your dreadful ideas.

[KIRILOV *disappears suddenly.* SHATOV *stares after him. There is a knock at the door.* LYAMSHIN *comes in.*]

SHATOV: I can't receive you now.

LYAMSHIN: I have something to tell you. I have come to tell you from Verkhovensky that everything is arranged. You are free.

SHATOV: Is that true?

LYAMSHIN: Yes, absolutely free. You will just have to show Liputin the place where the press is buried. I shall come to get you tomorrow at exactly six o'clock, before dawn.

SHATOV: I'll come. Now go. My wife has come back. [LYAMSHIN *leaves.* SHATOV *goes back towards the room.* MARIA *has gone to sleep. He places the tray on the table and watches her.*] Oh, how beautiful you are!

MARIA [*waking up*]: Why did you let me go to sleep? I'm in your bed. Ah! [*She stiffens as if in a sort of attack and grips* SHATOV*'s hand.*]

SHATOV: You are suffering, my dear. I shall call the doctor . . . Where does it hurt? Do you want compresses? I know how to make them . . . .

MARIA: What? What do you mean?

SHATOV: Nothing . . . I don't understand you.

MARIA: No, it's nothing. . . . Don't stand still. Tell me something. . . . Talk to me of your new ideas. What are you preaching now? You can't keep yourself from preaching; it's in your nature.

SHATOV: Yes. . . . That is . . . I am preaching God now.

MARIA: And yet you don't believe in Him. [*New attack.*] Oh, how unbearable you are! [*She repulses* SHATOV, *who is bending over the bed.*]

SHATOV: Maria, I'll do what you want. . . . I'll keep moving. . . . I'll talk.

MARIA: But don't you see that it's begun?

SHATOV: Begun? What has?

MARIA: Don't you see that I'm about to give birth? Oh! Cursed be this child! [SHATOV *gets up.*] Where are you going, where are you going? I forbid you!

SHATOV: I'll be back, I'll be back. We need money and a midwife.... Oh, Maria!... Kirilov! Kirilov!

[BLACKOUT. *Then the light gradually increases in the room.*]

SHATOV: She's in the next room with him.

MARIA: He is beautiful.

SHATOV: What a great joy!

MARIA: What shall I name him?

SHATOV: Shatov. He is my son. Let me fix your pillows.

MARIA: Not like that! How awkward you are! [*He does his best.*]

MARIA [*without looking at him*]: Lean over me! [*He leans towards her.*] Closer! Closer! [*She slips her arm around his neck and kisses him.*]

SHATOV: Maria! My love!

[*She rolls on her side.*]

MARIA: Ah! Nicholas Stavrogin is a wretch. [*She bursts into sobs. He caresses her and talks to her softly.*]

SHATOV: Maria. It's over now. The three of us will live together calmly, and we shall work.

MARIA [*reaching out and grasping him in her arms*]: Yes, we shall work, we shall forget everything, my love...

[*There is a knock at the door of the living-room.*]

MARIA: What's that?

SHATOV: I had forgotten it. Maria, I must leave you. I'll be gone a half-hour.

MARIA: You are going to leave me alone? We have just found each other after all these years and you are leaving me...

SHATOV: But this is the last time. After this we shall be together for ever. Never, never again shall we think of the horror of the past.

[*He kisses her, takes up his cap, and gently closes the door. In the living-room* LYAMSHIN *is waiting for him.*]

SHATOV: Lyamshin, have you ever been happy in your life?

[BLACKOUT. *Then* LYAMSHIN *and* SHATOV *step around the curtain representing the street.* LYAMSHIN *stops and hesitates.*]

SHATOV: Well! What are you waiting for? [*They continue walking.*]

BLACKOUT

SCENE NINETEEN

The Forest of Brykovo. SHIGALOV *and* VIRGINSKY *are already there when* PETER VERKHOVENSKY *arrives with* THE SEMINARIST *and* LIPUTIN.

PETER [*lifts his lantern and looks at them all in the face*]: I hope you haven't forgotten what was agreed.

VIRGINSKY: Listen. I know that Shatov's wife came back to him last night and that she gave birth to a child. Anyone who knows human nature knows that he will not denounce us now. He is happy. Perhaps we could postpone this for the present.

PETER: If you suddenly became happy, would you postpone accomplishing an act of justice that you considered just and necessary?

VIRGINSKY: Certainly not. Certainly not. But ...

PETER: You would prefer to be unhappy rather than to be cowardly?

VIRGINSKY: Certainly . . . I should prefer it.

PETER: Well, let me point out to you that Shatov now considers this denunciation just and necessary. Besides, what happiness could there possibly be in the fact that his wife, after an escapade of three years, has returned to him to give birth to a child by Stavrogin?

VIRGINSKY [*interrupting*]: Yes, but I protest. We'll ask him to give his word of honour. That's all.

PETER: You can't talk of honour unless you're in the pay of the government.

LIPUTIN: How dare you? Which of us here is in the pay of the government?

PETER: You, perhaps. . . . Traitors are always afraid at the moment of danger.

SHIGALOV: Enough, I must speak up. Since last night I have scrupulously examined the question of this assassination and have reached the conclusion that it was useless, frivolous, and petty. You hate Shatov because he despises you and he insulted you all. That is a personal question. But personal questions lead to despotism. Hence I am leaving you. Not out of fear of danger nor out of friendship for Shatov, but because this assassination contradicts my system. Farewell. As for denouncing you, you know that I won't do it. [*He wheels about and goes away.*]

PETER: Stay here! . . . We'll catch up with that madman. Meanwhile, I must tell you that Shatov already told Kirilov of his intention of denouncing us. It was Kirilov who told me, because he was shocked by it. Now you know everything. And, furthermore, you have taken an oath. [*They look at one another.*] Good. Let me remind you that we are to throw him into the pond afterwards and then scatter. Kirilov's letter will cover all of us. Tomorrow I am leaving for St Petersburg. You will have news from me soon. [*A shrill whistle. After a hesitation* LIPUTIN *answers it.*] Let's hide.

[*They all hide except* LIPUTIN. LYAMSHIN *and* SHATOV *come on stage.*]

SHATOV: Well! You are silent? Where is your pickaxe? Don't be afraid. There's not a soul here. You could shoot a cannon off here and no one would hear a thing in the suburb. Here it is. [*He strikes the ground with his foot.*] Right here.

[THE SEMINARIST *and* LIPUTIN *leap on him from the rear, seize his arms, and pin him to the ground.* PETER VERKHOVENSKY *puts his revolver to* SHATOV'*s forehead.* SHATOV *utters a brief, desperate cry:* 'Maria!' VERKHOVENSKY *shoots.* VIRGINSKY, *who has not taken part in the murder, suddenly begins to tremble and to scream.*]

VIRGINSKY: That's not the way. No, no. That's not the way at all.... No ... [LYAMSHIN, *who has stood behind him all the time without taking part in the murder either, suddenly grabs him from behind and begins screaming.* VIRGINSKY, *in fright, tears himself away.* LYAMSHIN *throws himself on* PETER VERKHOVENSKY, *screaming likewise. He is seized and silenced.* VIRGINSKY *weeps.*] No, no, that's not the way ...

PETER [*looking at them with scorn*]: Filthy cowards!

BLACKOUT

SCENE TWENTY

The street. VERKHOVENSKY, *hastening towards the Filipov lodging-house, encounters* FEDKA.

PETER: Why the hell didn't you stay hidden, as I had ordered you to?

FEDKA: Don't talk that way to me, you little sneak. I didn't want to compromise Mr Kirilov, who is an educated man.

PETER: Do you or don't you want a passport and money to go to Petersburg?

FEDKA: You are a louse. That's what I think you are. You promised me money in the name of Mr Stavrogin to shed innocent blood. I know now that Mr Stavrogin was not informed. So that the real murderer is neither me nor Mr Stavrogin: it's you.

PETER [*beside himself*]: You wretch, I'll hand you over to the police at once! [*He takes out his revolver. Quicker than he,* FEDKA *strikes him four times on the head.* PETER *falls.* FEDKA *runs away with a burst of laughter.* PETER *picks himself up.*] I'll find you at the other end of the world. I'll crush you. As for Kirilov!... [*He runs towards the Filipov lodging-house.*]

BLACKOUT

SCENE TWENTY-ONE

The Filipov lodging-house.

KIRILOV [*in complete blackness*]: You killed Shatov! You killed him! You killed him! [*The lights come up gradually.*]

PETER: I have explained it a hundred times. Shatov was on the point of denouncing us all.

KIRILOV: Shut up. You killed him because he spat in your face in Geneva.

PETER: For that. And for many other things too. What's the matter with you? Oh ...

[KIRILOV *has taken out a revolver and is aiming at him.* PETER VERKHOVENSKY *takes out his revolver too.*]

KIRILOV: You had got your weapon ready in advance because you were afraid I would kill you. But I'll not kill. Although ... although ... [*He continues taking aim. Then he lowers his arm, laughing.*]

PETER: I knew you wouldn't shoot. But you took a big risk. *I* was going to shoot ...

[*He sits down again and pours himself some tea with a trembling hand.* KIRILOV *lays his revolver on the table, starts walking up and down, and stops in front of* PETER VERKHOVENSKY.]

KIRILOV: I'm sorry about Shatov.

PETER: So am I.

KIRILOV: Shut up, you wretch, or I'll kill you.

PETER: All right. I don't regret him. ... Besides, there's not much time. I must take a train at dawn and cross the frontier.

KIRILOV: I understand. You are leaving your crimes behind and taking shelter yourself. Filthy swine!

PETER: Filth and decency are just words. Everything is just words.

KIRILOV: All my life I wanted there to be something other than words. That's what I lived for, so that words have a meaning, so that they would be deeds also ...

PETER: And so?

KIRILOV: So ... [*He looks at* PETER VERKHOVENSKY.] Oh, you're the last man I shall ever see. I don't want us to separate in hatred.

PETER: I assure you that I have nothing against you personally.

KIRILOV: We are both miserable wretches, and I am going to kill myself and you will go on living.

PETER: Of course I shall go on living. *I* am a coward. It's despicable, I know.

KIRILOV [*with increasing excitement*]: Yes, yes, it's despicable. Listen. Do you remember what Christ Crucified said to the thief who was dying on his right hand? 'Today shalt thou be with me in Paradise.' The day ended, they died, and there was neither Paradise nor Resurrection. And yet He was the greatest man on earth. Without that man the whole planet and everything on it is simply meaningless. Well, if the laws of nature did not even spare such a man, if they forced Him to live in lies and to die for a lie, then this whole planet is but a lie. What is the good of living, then? Answer, if you are a man.

PETER: Yes, what is the good of living! I have understood your point of view completely. If God is a lie, then we are alone and free. You kill yourself and prove that you are free and there is no God. But for that you must kill yourself.

KIRILOV [*more and more excited*]: You have understood. Ah! Everyone will understand if even a low scoundrel like you can understand. But someone has to begin and kill himself to prove to others the terrible freedom of man. I am unfortunate because I am the first and because I am dreadfully frightened. I am Tsar only for a short time. But I shall begin and open the door. And all men will be happy; they will all be Tsars and for ever. [*He rushes to the table.*] Ah! Give me the pen. Dictate and I'll sign anything. Even that I killed Shatov. Dictate. I don't fear anyone; everything is a matter of indifference. All that is hidden will be known, and you will be crushed. I believe. I believe. Dictate.

PETER [*leaps up and places paper and pen in front of* KIRILOV]: I, Alexey Kirilov, declare . . .

KIRILOV: Yes. To whom? To whom? I want to know to whom I'm making this declaration.

PETER: To no one, to everyone. Why specify? To the whole world.

KIRILOV: To the whole world! Bravo. And without repenting. I don't want any repenting. I don't want to address myself to the authorities. Go ahead, dictate. The universe is evil. I'll sign.

PETER: Yes, the universe is evil. And down with the authorities! Write.

KIRILOV: Wait a minute! I want to draw on the top of the page a face sticking out its tongue.

PETER: No. No drawing. The tone is enough.

KIRILOV: The tone – yes, that's it. Dictate the tone.

PETER: 'I declare that this morning I killed the student Shatov in the woods for his betrayal and his denunciation in the matter of the proclamation.'

KIRILOV: Is that all? I want to insult them too.

PETER: That's enough. Give it to me. But you haven't dated it or signed. Sign it now.

KIRILOV: I want to insult them.

PETER: Put down 'Long live the Republic.' That'll get them.

KIRILOV: Yes. Yes. No, I'm going to put: 'Liberty, equality, fraternity, or death.' There. And then in French: '*gentilhomme, séminariste russe et citoyen du monde civilisé.*' There! There! It's perfect. Perfect. [*He gets up, takes the revolver, and runs and turns out the lamp. The stage is in complete darkness. He shouts in the darkness at the top of his lungs*] At once! At once!

[*A shot rings out. Silence. Someone can be heard groping in the darkness.* PETER VERKHOVENSKY *lights a candle and casts a light on* KIRILOV'*s body.*]

PETER: Perfect! [*he goes out.*]

MARIA SHATOV [*shouting on the landing*]: Shatov! Shatov!

BLACKOUT

THE NARRATOR: Denounced by the weak Lyamshin, Shatov's murderers were arrested, except for Verkhovensky, who at that moment, comfortably installed in a first-class carriage, was crossing the frontier and outlining new plans for a better society. But if such as Verkhovensky are immortal, it is not certain that such as Stavrogin are.

SCENE TWENTY-TWO

At Varvara Stavrogin's. VARVARA STAVROGIN *is putting on a cape. Beside her,* DASHA *is wearing mourning.* ALEXEY YEGOROVICH *is at the door.*

VARVARA: Prepare the carriage! [ALEXEY *leaves.*] To run away like that at his age, and in the rain! [*She weeps.*] The fool! The fool! But he is ill now. Oh! I'll bring him back dead or alive! [*She starts towards the door, stops, and comes back towards* DASHA.] My dear, my dear! [*She kisses her and leaves.* DASHA *watches her from the window, then goes and sits down.*]

DASHA: Protect them all, good Lord, protect them all before protecting me too. [STAVROGIN *suddenly enters.* DASHA *stares at him fixedly. Silence.*] You have come to get me, haven't you?

STAVROGIN: Yes.

DASHA: What do you want with me?

STAVROGIN: I have come to ask you to leave with me tomorrow.

DASHA: I will! Where shall we go?

STAVROGIN: Abroad. We shall settle there for good. Will you come?

DASHA: I'll come.

STAVROGIN: The place I am thinking of is lugubrious. At the bottom of a ravine. The mountain cuts off the view and crushes one's thoughts. It is the one place in the world that is most like death.

DASHA: I'll follow you. But you will learn to live, to live again. . . . You are strong.

STAVROGIN [*with a wry smile*]: Yes, I am strong. I was capable of being slapped without saying a word, of overpowering a murderer, of living in dissipation, of publicly confessing my downfall. I can do anything. I have infinite strength. But I don't know where to apply it. Everything is foreign to me.

DASHA: Ah, may God give you just a little love, even if I am not the object of it!

STAVROGIN: Yes, you are courageous; you will be a good nurse! But, let me repeat, don't let yourself be taken in. I have never been able to hate anything. Hence, I shall never love. I am capable only of negation, of petty negation. If I could believe in something, I could perhaps kill myself. But I can't believe.

DASHA [*trembling*]: Nicholas, such a void is faith or the promise of faith.

STAVROGIN [*looking at her after a moment of silence*]: Hence, I have faith. [*He straightens up.*] Don't say anything. I have something to do now. [*He gives a strange little laugh.*]

What weakness to have come for you! You were dear to me, and in my sorrow it was pleasant to be with you.

DASHA: You made me happy by coming.

STAVROGIN [*stares at her with an odd look*]: Happy? All right, all right. . . . No, it isn't possible. . . . I bring nothing but evil. . . . But I'm not accusing anyone.

[*He goes out on the right. Hubbub outside.* VARVARA *comes in upstage. Behind her,* STEPAN TROFIMOVICH *is carried like a child by a tall, stalwart peasant.*]

VARVARA: Quick, put him on this sofa. [*To* ALEXEY YEGOROVICH] Go and get the doctor. [*To* DASHA] You, get the room warmed up. [*After laying* STEPAN *on the sofa, the peasant withdraws.*] Well! You poor fool, did you have a good walk? [*He faints. Panic-stricken, she sits down beside him and taps his hands.*] Oh, calm yourself, calm yourself! My dear! Oh, tormentor, tormentor!

STEPAN [*lifting his head*]: *Ah, chère! Ah, chère!*

VARVARA: No, just wait, keep quiet.

[*He takes her hand and squeezes it hard. Suddenly he lifts* VARVARA'*s hand to his lips. Gritting her teeth,* VARVARA STAVROGIN *stares at a corner of the room.*]

STEPAN: I loved you . . .

VARVARA: Keep quiet.

STEPAN: I loved you all my life, for twenty years . . .

VARVARA: But why do you keep repeating: 'I loved you, I loved you'? Enough. . . . Twenty years are over, and they'll not return. I'm just a fool! [*She rises.*] If you don't go to sleep again, I'll . . . [*With a sudden note of affection*] Sleep. I'll watch over you.

STEPAN: Yes. I shall sleep. [*He begins raving, but in an almost reasonable way.*] *Chère et incomparable amie,* it seems to me . . . yes, I am almost happy. But happiness doesn't suit me, for right away I begin to forgive my enemies. . . . If only I could be forgiven too.

VARVARA [*deeply moved and speaking bluffly*]: You will be forgiven. And yet . . .

STEPAN: Yes. I don't deserve it, though. We are all guilty. But when you are here, I am innocent as a child. *Chère*, I have to live in the presence of a woman. And it was so cold on the road. . . . But I got to know the people, I told them my life.

VARVARA: You spoke about me in your taverns!

STEPAN: Yes . . . but only by allusion . . . you see. And they didn't understand a word. Oh, let me kiss the hem of your frock!

VARVARA: Stay still. You will always be impossible.

STEPAN: Yes, strike me on the other cheek, as in the Gospels. I have always been a wretch. Except with you.

VARVARA [*weeping*]: With me too.

STEPAN [*getting excited*]: No, but all my life I've lied . . . even when I told the truth. I never spoke with the truth in mind, but solely with myself in mind. Do you realize that I am lying even now, perhaps?

VARVARA: Yes, you are lying.

STEPAN: That is. . . . The only true thing is that I love you. As for all the rest, yes, I am lying, that's certain. The trouble is that I believe what I say when I lie. The hardest thing is to go on living and not to believe in one's own lies. *Mais vous êtes là, vous m'aiderez* . . . [*He swoons.*]

VARVARA: Come back to life! Come back to life! Oh, he is burning hot! Alexey!

[ALEXEY YEGOROVICH *enters.*]

ALEXEY: The doctor is coming, madame.

[ALEXEY *goes out on the right.* VARVARA *turns back towards* STEPAN.]

STEPAN: *Chère, chère, vous voilà!* I reflected on the road and I understood many things ... that we should give up negating. We should never negate anything again.... It's too late for us, but for those to come, the young who will take our place, *la jeune Russie* ...

VARVARA: What do you mean?

STEPAN: Oh! Read me the passage about the swine.

VARVARA [*frightened*]: About the swine?

STEPAN: Yes, in St Luke, you know, when the devils enter into the swine. [VARVARA *goes to get the Gospels on her desk and leafs through them.*] Chapter VIII, verses 32 to 36.

VARVARA [*standing near him and reading*]: '... Then went the devils up out of the man, and entered into the swine: and the herd ran violently down a steep place into the lake, and were choked.

'And when they that fed them saw what was done, they fled, and went and told this in the city and in the country.

'Then they went out to see what was done; and came to Jesus, and found the man, out of whom the devils were departed, sitting at the feet of Jesus, clothed, and in his right mind: and they were afraid.'

STEPAN: Ah, yes! Yes.... Those devils who depart from the sick man, *chère*, you see – well, you recognize them.... They are our defects, our impurities, of course, and the sick man is Russia.... But the impurities leave him, they enter into the swine. I mean us, my son, the others, and we run violently down a steep place as if possessed of the devil, and we shall perish. But the sick man will be cured and he will sit at the feet of Jesus and all will be cured.... Yes, Russia will be cured some day!

VARVARA: You're not going to die. You say that just to torment me a little more, cruel man ...

STEPAN: No, *chère*, no.... Besides, I shall not die altogether.

We shall be raised from the dead, we shall be raised from the dead, won't we? If God is, we shall be raised. . . . That is my profession of faith. And I make it to you whom I loved . . .

VARVARA: God *is*, Stepan Trofimovich. I assure you that he exists.

STEPAN: I realized that on the road . . . amidst my people. I have lied all life long. Tomorrow, tomorrow, *chère*, we shall live again together . . . [*He falls back dead.*]

VARVARA: Dasha! [*Then, standing stiffly*] *O, mon Dieu,* have pity on this child!

ALEXEY [*rushing out of the room on the right*]: Madame, madame! . . . [DASHA *comes on.*] There! Look there! [*He points to the room.*] Mr Stavrogin!

[DASHA *runs towards the room. A gasp is heard from her. Then she comes out slowly.*]

DASHA [*falling on her knees*]: He has hanged himself.

[*The* NARRATOR *enters.*]

THE NARRATOR: Ladies and gentlemen, one word more. After Stavrogin's death the doctors conferred and pronounced that he showed not the slightest sign of insanity.

CURTAIN

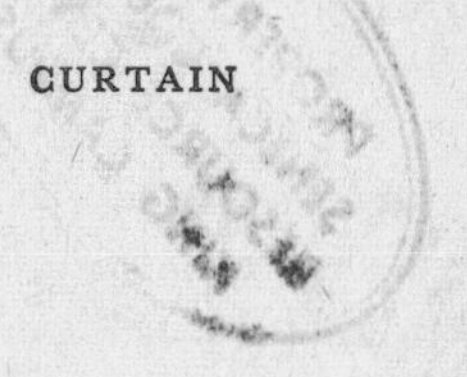